SECRET MEMOIRS OF A
BORN-AGAIN PREACHER

All proceeds from the sale of this book
will be donated to the
Guavio Elementary School
located in the oriental hills of Bogotá, Colombia

Guavio Elementary School serves boys and girls from eight neighborhoods, children of humble parents who work at menial jobs: bricklayers, mechanics, street sweepers, street vendors, garbage collectors, and kitchen servants. Most homes have at least one parent absent.

Guavio Elementary is a place of salvation for these children because their parents, so preoccupied by their long day's work, cannot devote much time to their offspring. The children suffer the effects of poor health due to poverty and lack of sufficient nutrition.

Right now, in 2011, there are 180 children attending Guavio Elementary, from pre-school through fifth grade. They have six teachers total. What they need most are books, writing implements, shoes, uniforms, and prizes for those who excel in their schoolwork.

SECRET MEMOIRS OF A BORN-AGAIN PREACHER

A satire by
Andrés Berger-Kiss

DANCING MOON PRESS
NEWPORT, OREGON

Secret Memoirs of a Born-Again Preacher
copyright © 2011 by Andrés Berger-Kiss
All rights reserved

This book is a work of fiction. Names, characters, places, and incidents
are the product of the author's imagination or are used fictitiously,
and any resemblance to actual persons, living or dead, business estab-
lishments, events, or locales is entirely coincidental.
But aren't all satires based on facts?

ISBN: 978-1-892076-93-9
Library of Congress Control Number: 2011933545
Berger-Kiss, Andrés
Secret Memoirs of a Born-Again Preacher
1. Title; 2. Fiction; 3. Satire; 4. Religion; 5. Ministerial studies;
6. Evangelization—Latin America; 7. Politics; 8. Sociopathic
development; 9. Pathological family relationships.

Author photo courtesy of Carla Perry
Book design: Carla Perry, Dancing Moon Press
Cover design & production: Dan Mandish, Mandish Design
Manufactured in the United States of America

DANCING MOON PRESS
P.O. Box 832, Newport, OR 97365, 541-574-7708
info@dancingmoonpress.com
www.dancingmoonpress.com

FIRST EDITION

Dedicated to all those
who have been bamboozled

Additional books by Andrés Berger-Kiss

Novels

Children of the Dawn
Hijos de la madrugada

Tomorrow's Promise
La promesa del mañana

Don Alejandro and His 186 Children
Donalejo y sus 186 hijos

Poetry

Voices from the Earth
Voces de la Tierra

My Three Homelands and A Fistful of Dust
Mis tres patrias y Un puñado de polvo

Short Stories

The Sharpener and Other Stories (an anthology)
Cartas a mi amante y otros cuentos de la vida

Translations from Spanish to English

Surgido de la luz, poetry by Nelson Romero Guzmán
Sprung from the Light (English by A. Berger-Kiss)

SECRET MEMOIRS OF A BORN-AGAIN PREACHER

1

My fascination with preaching began when Sister Todd, also known as The Reverend Sister Todd, converted me. From the moment I was born until I was an adolescent, we were together.

At one time The Reverend Sister Todd had great power among the faithful in the Midwest but, by the time we met, I was her only audience. Pretending to still be preaching in the revival tents, she let loose—for my benefit only—her formidable interpretations of the *Book of Revelation*. The Reverend was also my Grandma.

If I cried, she'd yell her sermon louder to cover the sounds I made until I would be startled into silence by the thunder of her booming voice. I didn't understand a word she said. I heard only her pronouncements, her oceanic sighs, and felt her hot tears dropping on my face. During the final apocalyptic movements of her declamatory binges, when her enormous body shook like an earthquake, I clung to her for dear life, my ear tightly pressed against her breast, listening to the pounding of her great evangelist's heart.

I learned early that words are secondary. What matters is the intensity. That was my first lesson as a preacher. In her arms, I was born again for the first time just about five years after my original birth.

My new life began soon after I took some of Grandmother's favorite goodies out of the cookie jar without her permission. I had finished my fourth cookie when she barged into the room, singing in her contralto voice, "The Tempter Tries Me Hard, but a Little Talk with Jesus Makes It Right." She continued singing while she looked at me and then at the jar on the windowsill. In a second she took in the significance of the whole scene: I had taken some of her cookies! I knew I had done something to displease her. I remember her arm stiffly outstretched toward the ceiling, her eyes staring beyond the wall, probably fixed upon the Promised Land. Slowly, the full strength of her glare moved toward me and reached the most recondite and secret place in my soul. Her agitated voice reverberated throughout the room. "I am the Alpha and the Omega, the First and the Last, the Beginning and the End! Now tell me, Dicky, did you eat some of my cookies? It's a sin to steal and it's a sin to lie. Either way the fires of Hell will burn the flesh off your bones till the end of Time!"

She let the notion of infinite punishment by fire sink into me and, realizing that I was in an impossible conflict, offered me a way out: "Confess your sin, be born again, and you won't burn in Hell." I had been burned before when I had touched the hot stove and was more afraid of fire than anything else in the world. Right then and there, I began to build a thick protective barrier around the place where threats could never hurt me while she tried to scare the bejesus out of me. I didn't understand the business about 'infinite' but got some idea of its meaning when she said I'd suffer day after day forever more. I wasn't about to take any chances, so I confessed my theft and learned my second lesson: you can bring people down by threatening them with fire! I had seen many get born again at revivals and had watched them cry before falling on their knees, asking for forgiveness. So I cried, to gain her approval.

Other than preaching to me, Granny was pretty aloof and left me alone most of the time. She was in charge of me because no one else, least my mother, wanted to bother with a child. My father, Reverend Todd's son-in-law, needing a cook and someone to clean house, gave her a place to stay with our family, on the condition she stop making public speeches and dedicate herself to the care of his household.

Once in a while my mother would stick a bone, soaked in steak juice, in my mouth, to shut me up. I'd chew on it until my gums bled. Granny scolded her and got me regular pacifiers, but by the time she thought of the alternative, I had learned to bite so hard that I'd chew up most of them.

"If you chew this one and wreck it, you don't get no

more. It's back to the bone for you," she'd say. Granny
told me much later that her threats hadn't worked, so she
got for me the toughest bones she could find. I think I
had bones in my mouth until I was eight. Since everyone
left me alone, these bone pacifiers were my only true
companions and they helped me fall asleep.

I gave up on both of them, Mom and Grandma, by
the time I could speak. I was not there as far as Mom was
concerned and I was a doll to Granny. In fact, that's what
she called me, "my pretty-boy-doll." But at least she
cuddled me once in a while.

Many anecdotes about Grandmother Todd's life were
revealed to me during my childhood and adolescence. She
had such strange ways that people remembered in great
detail what she said and did.

Before World War II, the Reverend Sister Todd was
famous throughout the plains of the Midwest as a young
fire and brimstone evangelist. Those who booked
preachers for revival meetings liked her passionate sermons and her outspoken ways of exposing the Federal
Government's shortcomings. They enjoyed the accusations she haphazardly hurled to the chanting mobs that
came to listen to her.

"The thugs in Washington will be punished in the
life to come for over-regulating the affairs of the free
people of our nation!"

"Amen, Sister, amen!" came back the chorus of parishioners.

"They're nothing but a dumb army of burros—
burrocratic burros, interfering with the God-given rights
of common citizens like us!" she proclaimed, getting big
laughs every time she reduced government employees to
the level of animals.

"Amen, hallelujah!" the congregation answered.

"Them perverts have nothin' better to do than stick
their grimy paws into our hard-earned money and turn it
into taxes for their upkeep!"

"Amen, amen, amen!" The roar would subside only
after she extended both arms, calming the worshippers.

Reverend Sister Todd didn't bother with local affairs,
concentrating her wrath solely on what she thought happened in Washington, D. C. "The Feds shouldn't meddle
in States' rights," was about as far as she commented on
issues relevant to Shawnee, our county.

By the time Franklin Delano Roosevelt got elected
president for the third time, she was sure he had his heart
set on becoming the first American emperor, bound to
establish a dynasty for his offspring.

A few of her faithful followers persuaded The Reverend to try her luck in the political arena, urging her to
straighten things out in Washington and fulfill the will of
the people. Secret collections were made and off she went
campaigning.

The Reverend met with the elders of her congregation and all decided, after a prayer meeting where they
asked guidance from Up Above, to go for the seat of the

youngest congressman. The fundamentalist churches organized and lobbied, cajoled and even threatened to form a third party unless she was selected. The Reverend took a run at a seat in the House of Representatives but failed to defeat the incumbent Democrat when someone told the press she had lied about her qualifications. She thought she could spice her résumé with a couple of made-up jobs and academic credentials.

"I lost the first round of a long battle. I am not one to give up easy. Wait till the next election, when I will expose those who spread vile lies about me! You'll see real action then! Abyssinia!" she declared.

As fate would have it, the unprecedented re-election of Roosevelt for a fourth term destroyed Grandmother Todd's last vestiges of sanity. She completely cracked on the day after the election.

Granny was put back together as well as they could at the intensive care unit of the Eastman wing of Topeka State Hospital, our local nut farm. Famed Menninger Clinic psychiatrists and psychologists, consultants who came to teach residents and interns at the State Hospital, studied her case carefully and came up with the diagnosis: "Acute Paranoid Reaction with Schizophrenic Disorder in a Schizo-Affective Personality," a complex label in vogue in those days. In simpler terms, it meant she was loonier than a bedbug, madder than a hatter. It also meant, in her case, that she had a short fuse.

As complex as the diagnosis sounded, it hadn't been

a difficult one to make when she said at the beginning of her examination, "It's the President's fault I'm here. That four-flushing son-of-a-bitch!"

"What president?" the psychiatrist, seated next to her at the head of the long conference table, inquired.

"Why, the President of these United States of America, of course."

"You don't care very much for the man, eh?"

"Abso-bloody-lutely not!"

"I see, but will you explain to us how did the president manage to accomplish that?" the man in the white coat asked while he studiously puffed on a curved pipe. There were many post-doctoral students around the table, plus a few nurses and a couple of occupational therapists. Some stared fish-eyed at the patient, some took notes.

Granny began to bawl abruptly, tears running down her chubby face, "Yes, with his new three-cent stamp." She wiped her tears with her hands and blew her nose into her skirt.

The psychiatrist questioning her lifted a hand and beamed his most beatific smile. "You don't have to say more if it's too painful for you. We'll understand."

"The old fart put the Feds up to doing me in all the way from Washington, D. C. with his three-cent Centenary of the Telegraph stamp." The Reverend dug into her pockets and pulled out a plug of tobacco. Looking around the room as though she had realized for the first time that she was in the midst of a meeting, surveying the field as it were, she continued, "I'll take a chaw if you don't mind."

"Go ahead." The psychiatrist smiled while she ripped off a piece of the tobacco with her teeth.

He narrowed his eyes, knitted his brow, sucked on his pipe, and scrutinized the ceiling as though the answer to his puzzlement might be scribbled up there somewhere among the cracks of the old building.

"Let me see if I get your meaning," he said, still absorbed in the ceiling, having now discovered a daddy-longlegs spider slowly crawling across it. He continued, pronouncing each word carefully, "The President of the United States, Mr. Roosevelt, wanted to harm you with a three-cent stamp?" He looked at the daddy-longlegs as he spoke, hoping it would not drop on his head, and then turned to Sister Todd.

The Reverend disregarded him as she suddenly stood up, looking all the while toward one of the psychology interns, a scholarly looking young man wearing thick glasses. She took a few steps in his direction and blurted out, "Stop lookin' daggers at me, Four Eyes! You're rattling my cage, you little dumb lout!"

"I was just paying attention, Sister Todd," the thin young man said in a high-pitched voice, carefully taking off his glasses. "I meant no offense."

The Reverend sauntered back to her chair with a disdainful look and stared at the interviewer. "You're no jayhawker but you're catching on, big boy!" she exclaimed.

"The stamps sent by the president through the U.S. Post Office had poisoned glue. The postal clerk who talked me into buying the stamps was the envoy. When I licked them stamps, my brain was fried by the poison and stopped working. That's how come I wound up in this spider-infested rat-hole with you! Now you know! I was poisoned by no other than F. D. R.!" She belched and made a wry face, adding, "See? I'm still burping up the damn stuff!"

Six months after her admission, Granny was discharged from the hospital. A nurse wrote in her case notes, "On the day of F.D.R.'s death, April 11, 1945, Sister Todd dropped her delusions!"

2

Preacher Todd was out of politics and out of a job, as well as out of the mental hospital. I was born the day after she was discharged, set loose again, just in time to welcome her when she returned home.

My grandmother was younger than my father was. He was in his late forties, a weather forecaster, who, one day, while looking at a tornado approach from the southwest and snake its way through the dusty Oklahoma panhandle into Kansas, was suddenly called from Above—way above the storm—to become a preacher.

He and my grandmother had shared the same pulpit for a few services before her hospitalization, urging people to come down to the altar, confess their sins and be saved, or face eternal damnation.

It was during Granny's stay at the hospital that my father married her pregnant daughter, Mildred, my mother. Mildred was barely fourteen, although my father told everyone she was over seventeen when they got married. Mildred used to call me "an unpleasant accident."

Dad, the Reverend James Paul Dink, came into the marriage a widower with a daughter Phyllis, who was six years older than I was.

My father was a good fisherman. "Fish or cut bait," he'd say to me when I was idle or uncertain about something. From the time I was four, Dad would take me and my sister Phyllis on fishing trips. He used us as bait to soften the hearts of the women he also brought along. Many said I was cute and fawned over me. Then, he'd take over. Phyllis and I were left in charge of the fishing poles while the two adults cavorted down the embankments through mud paths where they must have rolled on the ground, considering how they looked upon their return.

Preacher Dad ("P. D." as I began to call him shortly after I learned to read), spent much of his free time sitting on the crapper. It was his favorite place to read the magazines he called his journals.

Sometimes we'd run over to neighbors' houses, inventing excuses to use their bathroom. Ours was so often occupied by P. D. that I had to pee behind the old maple tree in our back yard. When I'd bang on the bathroom door, he'd say, "Can't you see I'm here on the pot, boy? Now, go on outside and pee on the maple tree!"

My sister Phyllis was more persistent. "What are you doing in there that's taking you so long?" she'd ask, making faces at the door.

"What you think I'm doin', eh?" he'd answer.

She'd wait a while, putting her ear against the door. "Are you still reading, Dad? C'mon, don't take all day! I also gotta pee, you know."

Even at the age of five, a vague thought began to stir in my brain, letting me know that things weren't quite right, that there was something different, about not only P. D. and Grandmother Todd, but also my entire family.

Granny read to me the *Holy Bible* from cover to cover, her plump finger faithfully touching each syllable as she clearly pronounced word for word the script she was reading. I don't know whether she meant to teach me how to read, pound the *Bible* into me, or simply didn't want to lose her place due to nearsightedness. I watched that finger with its long red nail bounce over the text while I listened, and that's how I learned to read before my fourth birthday. I hate to brag about it, but I was exactly three years and nine months old when I astounded everybody by reading impromptu from the *Bible* during Sunday School. That convinced everyone that I too must become a preacher, like the rest of my family. They said I had been called early for a special purpose.

Ever since I can remember, I wanted badly to be like King Solomon and repeat the words my grandmother thought were so beautiful. Deep down I felt that I was cut out to become a preacher!

In spite of my great intuitive power it took me years to figure it all out: How come I could read so early in life while my mother, at the age of twenty, was as illiterate as a doornail? As my mother aged, there was a change in her ways—the older she got, the less interest she took in anything except herself.

Nobody else existed for my mother. Only the face with pouting lips and hazy eyes, staring back at her from the mirror on the wall, kept her interest. She seductively tried out all kinds of poses, her thick lips painted with crimson and her green eyes heavily underlined with purple pencil.

Even now, after all these years, it's hard for me to deny the anger I felt toward Mildred. I began to call her Mildred shortly after my schooling started. To be so close to her, and yet so far, was more than I could endure. I thought at first that my mother hated me, but then I figured she really didn't care one way or another. Worse than to be hated is to be completely disregarded.

Mildred was in love with movie stars and often imitated her favorite ones. She used to dress up like the German actress, Marlene Dietrich. She'd lean back on a sofa in a low cut dress with a split skirt that showed off her long legs in front of that mirror and she'd slowly sing in a husky voice as she took a cigarette from her mouth, smoke floating all around her:

> It's not because I wouldn't.
> It's not because I shouldn't.
> And you know well it's not because I couldn't:
> It's only because I'm the laziest gal in town!

To be fair to Mildred, there was another interest she had that was much appreciated by everyone, perhaps the only attribute for which she might be remembered with gratitude. She was one hell of a good breakfast cook! Famished after ten hours of what she called her beauty rest, Mildred couldn't wait for anyone to make breakfast for her.

Every morning was banquet time! Mildred didn't step into the kitchen the rest of the day but, as a breakfast cook, was so good that everyone in the family, plus members of the congregation, and even the neighbors, managed to arrive uninvited in time to partake of her feasts. Grits and eggs with white beans, and side dishes of okra with hominy and cornbread were her specialty. For what she called her breakfast dessert, she cooked the most fantastic flapjacks bathed in maple syrup. She didn't serve anyone; she just prepared the food in large quantities. If you were lucky enough to be around to help yourself, that was OK by her.

"Smear yourself good with butter!" she'd admonish her customers. Just thinking about it makes my mouth water. To stay slim, she refrained from eating anything the rest of the day.

After I began to think for myself, I resented wanting her damn breakfasts. I didn't want to need anything from her. She was less crazy than Grandmother, but not nearly as soft. And stupid to boot. The only time I felt a measure of recognition from my mother was when she bragged about my good looks. But soon I realized that my value to her was that of an adornment.

My half-sister, Phyllis, was something else again. As far back as I can remember she eyed me with hostility. Huddled in a corner of the room, she'd stare at me for long periods as I lay in Granny's arms. Phyllis was mean to me and did things to torment me, like pinching me on the butt or arms when no one was looking, making sure she didn't leave any nail marks.

When my half-sister and I were alone, she'd rip the nursing bottle out of my mouth. I somehow caught on at the age of three that crying wouldn't do me any good. And I knew better than to give her the satisfaction of seeing me weep! She had been used to being the only child around our father, and my intruding into that arrangement displeased her.

Phyllis was freckle faced, with red hair flowing over her shoulders clear down to her knees. Most of the time she was withdrawn, but occasionally she'd hit me or hide one of my few toys. She was stubborn and usually did whatever she wanted to do. Strangely, as I grew older, I started looking up to her in spite of her cruelties. I hoped to be as strong as she was, even though I hated her.

When I was a little older, I discovered that if I held a magnifying glass over her pet cat, Tata, sleeping peacefully in the sunshine, it would jump and scream. I had great fun, laughing my head off at Tata's contortions, pretending the cat was Phyllis, but Tata grew to be afraid of me, running away screeching as soon as I'd come near. I lost interest in tormenting Phyllis's damn cat and fried a lot of ants, cockroaches and other crawly pests within my reach instead of bothering Tata.

My sister had acquired all the diseases of childhood and, with great regularity, she'd erupt with allergies. Her skin would break out at the slightest provocation—such as rain or dust, or even sunshine. When she was alone she'd press her two thumbnails against her face to get rid of her pimples. To look at Phyllis's face, neck and forehead after she had gone over every inch of skin with her thumbnails was not pleasant. Her face would be bloated after she was through with it. Until the swelling abated, she'd hide by placing a handful of her copious red hair over it. She'd sit there for hours, peering out through a slit of her hair with her small, brown eyes, sticking out her tongue at me when I'd look at her.

I didn't feel sorry for her the following year when she was bed-ridden with high fevers and moaned for hours. Fearing she might die, the congregation prayed around the clock on her behalf, asking the Lord to save her life. My parents weren't about to call in a doctor. Doctors didn't seem to favor our religion; none had joined our church, so there weren't any volunteers to cure my sister. My family wouldn't put out any money for professional consultations or medicine since they didn't believe in any of the sciences and people with advanced degrees were looked upon with suspicion.

"Let's wait for the prayers to help Phyllis get back on her feet," Mildred declared. "Those doctors would just take our money."

Luckily for Phyllis—and not so luckily for me, having prayed for her to die—she recovered. The credit for her recovery was given, of course, to the prayers by the faithful. When Phyllis's health improved, a special Thanksgiving service was held at our church.

"God works in mysterious ways," P. D. said.

Later on, my parents found out Phyllis had been afflicted with rheumatic fever. She would never be strong after that illness, and I was told that her two weeks of crisis might affect her heart as she grew older. I hoped she'd have less energy to harm me.

At thirteen, Phyllis was so underdeveloped that, had it not been for her long hair, you wouldn't have been able to tell whether she was a boy or a girl. At that age she began her acts of disappearance. We'd sometimes be sitting at the dining room table when she'd sneak out. Neither P. D.'s yelling for her nor did Mildred's threats impress her. Even Grandmother lost her patience.

Her absences increased so much that she was away most of the time, unavailable to do any of the chores, which, in her absence, were foisted on me. One day, when she skipped the short prayer meeting before dinner, P. D.—after whispering to the rest of us that he had found out where Phyllis was—yelled, "I know where you are, Phyllis. No use trying to hide."

Silence.

"You're in the basement lighting those damn matches. Now, come up before I go and get you, you brat!"

In the engulfing silence, the striking of a match in the basement could be heard. It was spooky!

"You've been stealing matches and I won't have any more of this nonsense. Come on up right now!" P. D. got up from the table and moved toward the basement trapdoor.

We heard the lighting of another match.

When Phyllis didn't respond, P. D. opened the trapdoor and rolled down a big log that was used to hold it open. The thundering log, bouncing down the steps and rolling through the basement floor, scared Phyllis out of her mind. She darted upstairs, her face flushed, screaming, "Help! Help! He wants to kill me! Help!"

Phyllis insisted that P. D. had tried to murder her that day. But I knew otherwise because, just before he rolled the log, he tiptoed toward us and whispered, "Shhh, I'm gonna scare the shit out of Phyllis. See if that'll work. She's hiding under the stairs."

It's obvious that one couldn't grow up in a family such as mine and remain unscathed. But so far I have managed well, thank you very much. Some people would say that my taking money from the Sunday School collection plates and exaggerating things might indicate the presence of trouble inside my head. But I've always maintained that I was just taking money I was more or less entitled to, and that truth has so many facets, it's really difficult to ascertain what is true and what is a lie. I figured what's good for me—especially if it feels good—is what counts.

Still, in my more introspective moments I can't help but feel there's one thing that has really disturbed me: knowing well that I would be stuck for life with the family's name—Dink! Why, oh why, did they baptize me as Richard?

When my classmates discovered they could make jokes using my name, there was no end to the shower of pestering ruining my days. And the teasing escalated as I advanced in school. From "Dinky," I went on to be called "Dicky Dink," and later on, "Dinky Dick." Every kid made up a different combination of names, hurling at me his own favorite variety. Of course, it gave me a chance to bust more than a couple of noses. But after a few such incidents, I lost some of the privileges I had in school and didn't have as much fun getting even with my fists. I preferred to outwit the bastards and get something they valued, such as baseball cards, candy or money. Still, I couldn't ever shake the teasing about my name. Such was the legacy that my family left for me.

3

Grandmother Todd had recited for me King Solomon's "Song of Songs" a hundred times plus. After the *Book of Revelation*, the *Old Testament* was her thing, especially following her hospitalization, where she encountered a Polish-Jewish psychiatrist, Doctor Targownikstein, who would become her psychotherapist on the ward.

Granny spoke to me many times about him. "He is a small guy but very strong, with a heavy foreign accent. I talked to him for hours and everything I said was important to him. When I left the hospital he put his hands on my shoulders—the only time he ever touched me—and told me never to preach again or talk about the Holy Ghost, to stay away from crowds, including church, and especially to stay out of the Post Office."

Granny often applied what she had learned in the hospital from Doctor Targownikstein. Through his teachings, she gave me a way to face the predicament my classmates placed me in with their constant teasing.

"That's a simple one. They're unhappy with the size

of their whang, Dicky," she informed me. "That's why they tease you. They get giddy just saying your name, believing you have more than they have." Little did I suspect then what a specialist my grandmother was on the subject of the dong. And metaphors.

This understanding of metaphors and symbols that Doctor Targownikstein had so skillfully implanted in her to ward off future bouts with madness became part of my early education. I got secondhand benefits, so to speak, that not only helped me put a protective shield between myself and my classmates, but also firmed up the sense of superiority I was developing.

For Grandmother, metaphors became the crux of her daily existence after her release from the hospital. At the slightest opportunity, she'd deliver a lecture to anyone who would listen. She'd say, "The original Hebrew writers of the *Bible's Old Testament* were a bunch of frustrated old men who screwed us women over with their demeaning version of *his*tory. Doctor Targownikstein reassured me. He told me he envied *me* for being able to do something no man can do: make babies! He'd say to me, 'Rheverent, you arh a factorhy, a pouverful factorhy! It is not the penis envy that afflicts poorh vomen, bahhh! It is the voomb envy that makes men crhazy!' I finally understood that we women have something for which men would give their eyeteeth. Why, I wouldn't be surprised if one of these days, they'll figure out a way to take that away from us too, and make babies in laboratories."

People listened transfixed to Sister Todd, not sure whether she still belonged in a lunatic asylum or was a prophet on the loose. Women came from all over town to listen to her discourses on Creation. I could see that one-on-one she was definitely better off than when a crowd gathered.

"The old men who wrote the Old Testament," she'd blurt out at the first available opportunity, "would have us believe that it was Eve who first tasted the forbidden fruit and went on to tempt Adam to take a bite also. Do you really believe that Eve, mother of us all, would let a stupid snake talk her into getting in trouble with the Lord? These old men who wrote the Book claimed that the serpent was more subtle than any beast of the field which Jehovah God had made. I'll tell you why they wrote that. Sisters, a serpent is nothing but a symbol for a penis. It was from a penis that the old men who wrote the *Bible* wanted the Power to come from."

In the presence of a larger audience, or even a couple extra people, Granny felt the old power that had been hers in the large tents of the revival meetings during steamy Kansas summers, where hundreds came down to the altar to be blessed by her and gain eternal salvation.

One afternoon P. D. held a revival meeting near our home, under a tent, on what had been a recently picked wheat field in the outskirts of Topeka. While the last rays of the baking sun made us feel like we lived in a bowl made of molten gold, a group of ladies, possibly in search of fresher air, sauntered over to our house. As soon as they came in the house, embracing Sister Todd, she was at it just like in the old days. Unable to control her passions, Granny felt again the surge inside her soul for a fleeting quarter of an hour. I saw that she was heading for trouble the minute she started. Whenever she began talking about the Holy Ghost, she was in deep shit.

When the women answered her last blessing, saying, "Amen, Amen," Granny admonished them, "That's something else I've been meaning to call to your attention. I'm tired of hearing, 'Amen, Amen.' We ought to say, 'Awomen, Awomen!' You hear?" Without giving anyone a chance to respond, she'd plunge into her next theme: "About Evolutionism, ol' Charlie Darwin didn't know shit from Shinola—pardon my French. Maybe *he* came from apes, the fowl-mouthed, no-good, son-of-a-bitch! We're no animals, sisters. The truth is the Divine light of Almighty Holy Ghost in Heaven shines in every one of our immortal souls. Hallelujah! Praise the Lord and the Holy Ghost! Awomen, yes! Excuse me, sisters, I gotta take a pit stop. I'll be right back."

The women looked at each other dumbfounded, fearful that Sister Todd was losing her marbles again. When Granny returned, one of the women got up from her chair and came over to Sister Todd with her arms open and spoke like someone addressing a child, "Have you been feeling OK, dear Reverend?"

Sister Todd put one hand out, stopping the intruder,

warning her, "Don't tread on me!" and went on un-
daunted, "With the help of the Holy Spirit I am re-writing
the Scriptures. To correct the old men's lies." She watched
the women squirming, starting to leave.

"You just wait a minute!" Granny nearly screamed.
"The worst part is how man was cursed later by God
because of us and made to work hard as punishment.
Look in your *Bible* and see how even their deaths are
blamed on us. A new version of the Scriptures must be
written and I will do it."

Granny's ambition to write was only wishful thinking. She didn't have the discipline to sit down and put
her thoughts on paper. She'd talk a mile a minute and
make a few attempts to harness what she rattled off with
such conviction, but no sooner than it would take her to
find a sheet of paper and place it on a desk, sharpen her
pencil, move the chair close and plunk herself down, her
mind would start wandering, and she'd get impatient
and begin talking again—even when she was by herself!
Nobody could match her when it came to gab, but as far
as sitting down to write, forget it. She had a bad case of
writer's block. That's how the years flicked by and the
new version of the Scriptures didn't get written.

Many itinerant salesmen of religious icons, faith healers
and born-again converts seeking to render their testimonials
showed up at our camp throughout the years. Most of
them were immediately sent packing by P. D., who had
no inclination to share even a minute of his pulpit time

with anyone. But a Reverend Alvin came to town with a great reputation among the preachers of the region for his ability to finagle more money from the parishioners than anyone thought possible. Reverend Alvin was the only one well received by P. D., and suddenly Mildred took an interest in singing solos to the congregation, especially when P. D. was gone and Reverend Alvin Grabbe, a handsome devil twice P. D.'s size, performed.

One odd thing about the newly appeared reverend was how he treated his dog, a large bitch hound, a mixture of many stray races. He had her wear diapers soaked in alcohol whenever she was in heat. When Mildred laughed at the sight of the diapered bitch, the reverend explained with a straight face, "When Candy's in heat, she has to wear those diapers soaked in alcohol so the horny males will be thrown off the scent and won't hump her. I gotta protect my investment." When he spoke he looked at people straight, without blinking, and his voice was mellow and seductive. He wore a permanent smile on his face.

Mildred played up to Reverend Alvin. I saw her making Marlene Dietrich eyes at him. Mildred went to church wearing a lot of gaudy, cheap jewelry and a long skirt with side-slits clear up to her thighs. Her face was heavily made up, with false eyelashes pasted on. She looked sexiest when singing the hymn "What a friend we have in Jesus" in the husky voice she used in front of the mirror.

An older lady in the congregation dared to confront Mildred, asking, "You think it's proper to dress like that in the House of God?" Mildred answered right off, swinging her hips, "I praise the Lord the best way I know how." With that answer the discussion was closed and I never saw that woman again. Everybody else either accepted the way Mildred looked or kept their traps shut. Once I was old enough to know about such things, Mildred looked to me like a cheap whore. But I learned a great lesson: No matter what you do, how extreme a thing you say, most any congregation is willing to forgive and forget and praise you, especially if you say that you're being moved by the Spirit.

The Reverend Alvin Grabbe liked Mildred. I saw him swallow saliva every time they met. Every time he had the pulpit, he gave her the opportunity to slink around, clinging to her microphone while she sang. When P. D. learned about her contributions to the services, he just shrugged his shoulders and said, "She's got a lot to offer." But as I could tell, P. D. and the new man became good friends.

Alvin Grabbe didn't fool me. Not even the first day I met him, when he brought to the house a bagful of Hershey kisses, the chocolate I liked so much. He came over to me with the bag in his hand, his eyes narrowing into a phony sweetness. He took out one of the small kisses, peeled the wrapper, held the delicious morsel of chocolate in front of my nose, and mellifluously said to me,

"Dicky boy, I want you to tell me who's the nicest man you know."

"The Reverend Alvin," I blurted out, adding the bit about Reverend to butter him up.

"That's a good boy! But you don't have to call me Reverend," he winked at me and nudged his elbow against my ribs. "That's only for the church people. You and me are gonna be buddies, Dicky." He popped me the piece of candy right away.

No sooner had I gobbled up the first kiss than he placed another one in front of my nose.

"And who's the most generous man you've ever met, Dicky boy?"

"You, Alvin, are the most generous man I've ever met."

By the third kiss, I hated the guts of the obnoxious bastard, yo-yoing me around like that for a measly piece of candy. But I was addicted to chocolate and would take as much as I could get.

I had a hint as to what he really wanted when, after emptying the bag, he said, "Now, Dicky boy, be sure to tell your mom what a wonderful time we had together, you hear? And next time I come I'll take you to the ice cream parlor."

While all this was going on, Granny just lay there with her arms spread out, probably over-medicated, snoring away, with me hugging her while munching the chocolate and burying my face in the folds of her vast bosom. I guess I behaved more like a three-year-old instead of the eight-year-old that I was.

Alvin became a regular visitor. P. D. didn't seem to mind. They split up the offerings collected at church meetings conducted by Alvin.

"Now, wait just a minute," Alvin would say to the collection crew. "Don't pass the plates in such a hurry. Give the men plenty of time to dig deep in their pockets, the women to empty their purses, while you look at them straight in the eyes, and your look will induce guilt in them if they're stingy. They know that others are also watching them, and that today they're giving to God Almighty, not to me, not to Reverend Daniel Paul Dink, but to the suffering Christ on the cross."

"So, how much was the take on Sunday?" P. D. asked Alvin after returning from one of his trips.

"Two hundred and twenty-six dollars and twelve cents, to be exact. Here's your one hundred and thirteen dollars and six cents, ol' buddy."

"That's the biggest offering this church ever had on a Sunday," P. D. answered, overwhelmed, looking in awe at all the bills in his hand. "Normally, they might drop fifty."

"Leave it to me, pal. Leave it to me. You need some lessons on how to arouse guilt to get the most you can."

4

By the time I turned nine, my fifteen-year-old half-sister Phyllis began to take on the shape of a girl. She refused to have her hair cut and it had grown almost to the floor. I saw her once undo her hair and prance around a chair in the dining room, nearly catching up to her trailing hair as she kept taking bigger steps until it got all tangled up in the furniture. It looked like a wave of fire behind her. She might have qualified to show it off in a circus. P. D. threatened to cut it short, saying it was a hazard and unhealthy besides. "You can't wash all of it, and bugs will nest there," he told her angrily.

"My hair is my own and I won't let anybody mess with it," she yelled back.

One time I was foolish enough to touch her hair out of curiosity. She turned around as fast as a tornado, slapped my hand and said, "I'll kill you if you do that again!"

I don't know what happened to Phyllis to make her so mean. Maybe it was due to her mom running off with a Fuller Brush door-to-door salesman, leaving no forwarding address. Phyllis was left to fend on her own, since P. D. treated her like air and they only came in contact when he wanted to discipline her. It had not worked out well.

I kept out of Phyllis's reach and made sure Granny protected me, because there was no telling what my sister might do next. She hardly ever looked at anybody straight in the eyes, except maybe while her hair covered her face, and she'd peek out between the strands. My favorite secret name for her was "Shifty Eyes." When she was angry, darts of hot hatred pierced through her veil of red hair. I was deeply envious of the way she could intimidate people by narrowing her small eyes and taking a one-shot look at them.

Soon after Phyllis hit fifteen, she began to take an interest in men. Not boys. Men in uniform especially attracted her. She wasn't too particular about what kind of uniform they wore. It could be a milkman in white clothes. She had a collection that could fill a barrel of cut out pictures from newspapers and magazines of men in uniform. She spent hours gazing at them, sorting them, reshuffling them, pasting them all over her room. She said it was her hobby. In fact, it was hard to tell whether she really liked the men or just their uniforms because she often cut the heads and hands of the men out of the pictures.

"Tata, I like Navy uniforms best," I heard her confide to her cat. She hardly spoke to any of us, but she had a soft heart for her cat. Tata was her best friend, her only friend. In the street she'd stop to pick up any stray kitten and talk to it like you might gab to a baby.

P. D. didn't like her bringing stray cats to her room. "Haven't I told you a hundred times not to bring these lice-infested beasts into the house?" he admonished her. "Out with it. Right now!"

If looks could kill, he'd have dropped dead on the spot.

One day, when the milkman, in his starched uniform, came up the porch steps, Phyllis undid her long hair, opened the door wide and stepped out on the porch without a stitch of clothes. The poor man quickly placed the milk bottles on the floor and took off. One of our neighbor ladies, who had seen the event, told P. D. about it. To teach her a lesson, finally finding an excuse to carry out what he had wanted to do for a long time, P. D. sneaked into her room late that night and, while she slept, cut her hair to an inch from her skull.

When Phyllis woke up in the morning, she started screaming as though she had lost her most valuable limb. Most of my sister had been hair up till then and losing it shocked the living daylights out of her. Shorn, she had no place to hide. I didn't feel an ounce of pity for her. Screaming, she began to desperately search for her lost hair. When she finally found her curls in the garbage can, she pulled them out and covered her nearly bald head with them, awash in tears, cursing and mumbling incoherently. Without hair, I could hardly recognize her. She looked so ridiculous, I almost burst out laughing, forcing myself to cough instead. Later on, she wrapped her arms and hands around her head and body, as though she were naked.

To get on her good side I said, "I'm truly sorry, Phyllis, you lost your beautiful hair."

She replied menacingly, "I don't want your pity, you half-wit."

It took Phyllis a month to get over her loss enough to go out of the house again, wearing a piece of cloth wrapped around her head like a turban. Good thing school hadn't started. After her initial explosion she said nothing about the haircut. But she never talked to P. D. again. He was invisible as far as she was concerned.

I think I was the only one—besides Phyllis—who remembered the date when P. D. cut her hair so short: August 1, 1955. I remembered because on that very day I was saved for the second time, out of conviction on this round, instead of fear.

It hadn't rained in Kansas for five months and everybody talked of nothing else but the need for rain. Out of the blue, Granny said to me, "My doll-boy, I bet if *you* started praying, the rain will come. And then you'll surely be saved more than you already are." She convinced me I was special!

"You really and truly think I can make it rain, Grandmother?" I asked her, wishing I could.

"Goodness gracious. No, child, not you. But if you

believe in your heart that God answers prayers, if you can pray as one who wants to be born again and again, ask the right way, God will bring the rain."

I got on my knees and raised my arms to the heavens, as she told me to do, and came up with a prayer.

"That's the most beautiful prayer I've ever heard, Dicky," she mumbled, sobbing.

"Did you take your medicine this morning?" I asked her, since I had never seen her cry so profusely.

"I'll take it later. I'm not depressed," she protested.

Outside, the Kansas sun was as potent as a furnace blazing in the clear sky. It had been like that since spring. The parched wheat fields were slowly brushed by waves of soft breezes that seemed to be omens of further heat. There was not even the tiniest cloud in the whole wide firmament. But no sooner than it took me to get up from my knees, we heard a rumbling thunder that came from beyond the straight line of the earth's curvature in the distant horizon. It was a very long and brooding sound. And half an hour later it was pouring rain from a dark sky.

"Praised be God Almighty!" Granny yelled. "Look at what's coming down from the very hand of God!" I was impressed with my own power. Granny embraced me, her tears running all over my face.

"Oh, the joy, child. The Power came from God to me and then to you through my blood and back again to God, oh the joy!" Grandmother was exultant. And so was I.

"Do you believe in your eternal salvation now, Dicky? Have you now been truly saved by the blood of the Lamb?"

"Praise the Lord, I have. I'm really saved, Grandma, I'm saved!"

I had never been too sure about the first time, but this time I had no doubts. I was so amazed at my own feat that I had to believe, but as time flicked on, my convictions weakened and by the time I was thirteen I developed real contempt for those who absurdly believed such things.

Those two important events—my sister losing her hair, and the power of my prayer—taking place on that first day of August, became engraved on the stone of my memory. On that day, exactly one year later, P. D. died. He was in bed with a bad case of the flu while Granny, Mildred and I went shopping. When we returned, half the Topeka Fire Department was at our house, poking around the still smoldering remains.

Phyllis returned in the evening and said she had been out with a uniform. I kept my observation about the day being a special anniversary to myself, and played dumb when Phyllis glared at me while she gave what I came to believe was an alibi. I knew better than to blabber my suspicion to anyone, especially since I didn't give a damn about P. D.

The Fire Chief's almost illegible, handwritten, rambling report in the Fire Department's logbook concluded as follows: "We found the body of the Reverend James Paul Dink burned crispier than a piece of overcooked Canadian bacon, sitting on the crapper, still holding on to a bunch of half-charred girlie magazines."

5

Pastors from the fundamentalist churches throughout Shawnee County were present at P. D.'s funeral. The men solemnly offered their prayers and made a few remarks about P. D. having been a good Christian, a pastor who took good care of his flock's needs. The longest and most effusive speech was made by Alvin, with Mildred looking at him with great admiration. Many of the mourners were women, and they were the ones who got most fired up, who testified in detail about how he had led them to the path of righteousness, and how much they were going to miss him, his comforting reassurances, his deeply felt convictions. But I knew that what they would really miss was whatever happened during their secret meetings behind the revival tents.

Mildred was hanging on Alvin's arm most of the time, showing off her customary array of shiny trinkets. She was dressed more for a party than a funeral. It was the first time I saw her wear ankle bracelets.

When I realized that genuine mourners were watching, feeling sorry for fatherless me, I tried to force myself to cry, but my eyes were as dry as buffalo turds cured by the sun in the scorched Kansas prairie. It would take me years to acquire the ability to cry at the drop of a hat, a skill which comes in handy for so many preachers.

Granny kept urging me to pray for my father and I muttered something, but I might as well have been reciting my multiplication tables. I felt nothing. I kept asking myself, especially as I watched most of the women bawling, if I shouldn't feel something for him. After all, he had been my father. And he had taken me fishing a few times, even though I was merely the bait he used to attract women. I knew I wasn't going to see him again, but I also knew I wasn't going to miss him. The grown-ups asked me if I wanted to put a handful of dirt on his grave to help bury him, so I picked up some earth and threw it into the hole right on top of his black coffin.

I was unmoved. I thought the handful of earth I had thrown in landed too hard; I noticed the hollow, wooden sound it made. I might have been burying a dead bird for all I cared. It was uncanny, but my father's burial liberated me from the feelings that make most people sad. I felt proud of my independence, not really being attached to anyone, feeling above those who were crying. I stood there and glared at the hole and the coffin, watching the clumps of dirt thud against the wood box.

I was aware of Phyllis during the whole funeral. She kept looking at me as though she were trying to divine whether I suspected her of any wrongdoing.

The daring pyromaniac!

I tried to stay as close to Granny as possible, out of my sister's view. But Phyllis kept her eyes glued on me. And now, without the torrent of red hair over her shifty peepers, she had a good look at me. I was intimidated by her, but I wasn't afraid.

"What's the matter, Doll?" Granny inquired as I used her as a shield.

"That piece of earth I threw in the hole must have packed a stone or something. It made such a horrible sound," I answered.

"Horse feathers! That was just dirt and grass you threw in. The sound was hollow because it was also the moment your Dad's blessed soul left his body empty, and the thud we heard was the wondrous sound of the Pearly Gates of Heaven opening to let your daddy pass through. We should all rejoice!"

Suddenly she screamed, "Rejoice, everyone!" while everybody stared at her. "The Reverend Dink has just crossed the Pearly Gates! Awomen!"

Granny looked at me and urged, "C'mon, Dicky boy, don't just stand there like a lump on a log, rejoice!"

Each person walked by P. D.'s graveside and dumped a handful or two of earth from the pile next to the big hole. We were in the middle of this ritual when a woman's frenzied voice broke through the prayers and rejoicing of the mourners. A middle-aged lady waddled in our direction, wailing most sorrowfully. She was huge, the folds of her flesh superimposed upon each other, her arms like short sides of beef poking out awkwardly from her enormous chest. She could not hold them normally by her side due to the abundance of flesh around her middle. Her legs stuck out from buttocks twice as large as the rest of her upper body. She took grotesque, miniature steps.

Intuitively, I knew who she was, watching her approach. Her small, brown eyes, imbedded in her bloated, anguished face, gave her away. She was Phyllis's mother, old P. D.'s first spouse.

My God, I thought, caught in a peculiarly childish type of illogic I must have picked up listening to Granny's discourses. If Phyllis is my half-sister and this lady is her mother, is she my half-mother?

Phyllis's mother arrived at the inner circle surrounding the grave, panting, and asked, nearly choking, "You are putting to rest the remains of the Reverend James Paul Dink?"

"Yes, ma'am," someone ventured.

"I knew it! I knew it!" she screamed. "And I never had a chance to see him again!" She fell on her knees and started bawling while she grabbed armfuls of dirt and heaved them into the grave. Then she started sobbing, "Forgive your bad wife for running out on you, for leaving our child. Forgive me!"

She took duck-like steps toward the grave and before the astonished eyes of the mourners leapt into it while screaming, "Forgive me, Pauley, forgive me!"

Two burly men scrambled into the grave to help her, while others went to get a ladder. It was like raising an elephant from a hole. Awash in tears, while she was being hoisted up, she plaintively looked at Granny and sobbed, "Elberta, Elberta, I know I've done him wrong, but I've repented, forgive me." I assumed correctly that Granny had been known as Elberta during her youth. She was, apparently, a woman of many moods and many names.

Granny turned to Phyllis's mother and said, "Why ask your old friend to forgive you, Floye? Ask your daughter. There she is." She pointed toward Phyllis, who had shifted her glaring eyes from me and was now gaping at this apparition lifted from the grave. Granny moved her head from side to side and added with a note of amazement in her voice, "You've sure grown pretty big, Floye, since I last seen ya."

Floye had been placed safely by the open grave, where she sat bruised and dirty, closely watched by a couple of our larger parishioners.

Overlooking the slight, Floye continued asking to be forgiven while she aimlessly tossed more dirt in the general direction of the coffin. As though she had just heard the reference to her daughter, Floye stopped and turned to Granny again, "Elberta, you mean to tell me that slender, red-haired girl over there is ... my Phyllis?"

Phyllis had always been unflappable. But this time she was truly great, cool as a cucumber, totally unmoved, making me feel even more envious. She was pure chill.

"Please forgive your mother, Phyllis, please," Floye kept hollering.

Nobody seemed to know what to do. Phyllis looked at Floye in a detached way and just stood there stiff as a petrified rock while Floye embraced her. Finally, Alvin saw his opportunity and saved the day. He came over and said, his honeyed voice spreading far beyond the circle of people who were attending the ceremony, "Those who ask forgiveness from the Lord first will be forgiven by Man."

Floye got on her knees again and screamed out, "I do! I do! I ask forgiveness from the Lord before all of you Christians. May my sins be forgiven!"

"Amen," said Alvin, blessing her, enjoying the encounter of mother and daughter after so many years, even though Phyllis hadn't said a word. Most of the mourners got on their knees to pray, but Phyllis remained standing, looking out in space.

After the commotion subsided, I could see Phyllis was staring at me again. I promised myself to stay out of her way, never to contradict her, and—especially—to always watch my back.

When Granny, Mildred, Phyllis and I moved into a small trailer, watching my back became a difficult chore. The only good thing to come out of the deal, as far as I could tell, was the ease with which we could access to the bathroom without P. D. monopolizing it.

Since neither P. D. nor Mildred believed in insurance, when the house burned down we lost everything.

The collection plates were passed around our own Light of God Church and several other fundamentalist churches like Brethren in Christ Assembly and The Church of the Anointed, but what came in fell short of the cost of a trailer.

While she stayed in Topeka, Floye followed Alvin like a wounded puppy wherever he went. I guess she was so grateful he had forgiven her sin that she forked out the rest of the money to buy a secondhand trailer for us. She said a windfall from an investment in pork belly futures in Chicago had recently brought her extra income. She returned to Chicago a couple of days later, saying she would come back to visit, a promise she never kept.

We all went to the Atchison, Topeka & Santa Fe railroad depot to see her off. But Phyllis didn't say a word to her.

"Aren't you even going to say good-bye to your mother?" Alvin asked her.

"She didn't say good-bye when she abandoned me," was all Phyllis answered.

"Learn to forgive, child, even if it's hard," Alvin admonished her to no avail. Phyllis could bear a grudge for life.

When the train began to move, Floye gave us the saddest look one could imagine and slowly waved her hand goodbye. She looked at Phyllis, tears flowing down her cheeks, and just before the train took her out of our sight she blew a kiss to her daughter. The rest of us waved back at Floye, but Phyllis just stood there frozen to the spot, not even looking in her direction.

6

I suspected that Mildred was involved with Alvin even before P. D. died. After the funeral, the two of them started fooling around in public like a couple of teenagers. But they were not devoted enough to get married. Alvin said he wouldn't let a woman take anything away from him, least of all his freedom to come and go as he pleased. "The only female I'll keep forever is my bitch Candy," he said with a smirk on his face. I had also heard him say on several occasions that he didn't like children.

For a while, Alvin took over P. D.'s function at the church, but he wasn't interested in becoming the permanent preacher for this congregation. I once heard him say to P. D., "They're willing to pay much more when you come in during an emergency, as a temporary preacher or for revivals. If they become too familiar with you, the first thing they do is hold the line on your salary and load you down with all kinds of extra work. Why, some of them would even have you move furniture. I firmly believe in the old saying, 'familiarity breeds contempt.' "

Alvin was a sort of freelancer making money off religion, filling in here and there but not staying with any one church for too long. He always left them wanting more.

P. D.'s congregation eventually found another full-time preacher, but nobody in my family attended services there again. I think the affair between Alvin and Mildred soured some of the folks in the church toward her.

After P. D.'s untimely death, my family heard of a small church on the other end of town, called The Light of the Holy Ghost Fundamental Parish, run by an octogenarian so besieged by the tremors of Parkinson's disease that he could barely hold the *Bible* in his hands. Someone had to help him walk from a chair to the pulpit, round trip. We attended his short sermons sporadically for about six months, until he died. The more he deteriorated, the shorter his sermons became, until toward the end he barely said anything. It's amazing how much a congregation will tolerate from a preacher.

When the Light of the Holy Ghost congregation began searching for a replacement, Granny let it be known that she was ready to make a comeback, even though she had not been to services in years, feeling that if she was not the leader she would not be a participant.

Mildred warned her, "Doctor T told you to stay away from preaching and crowds. Of course, I think..."

"End of discussion! I'm not interested in hearing what my daughter thinks, as though she had a brain to think with. If they'll have me, I'll do it. I have never been one to shy away from a challenge. Remember, I was a Republican candidate for Congress and the religious people—the fundamentalists—were all going to vote for me. Around here, that makes you a member of a very select group all your life, one in a million. Don't forget. And I haven't taken full advantage of that yet."

"Suit yourself. See if I care, Mother, if you...."

"Mother nothing! If they want me, I'll serve. They all know I'm cleaning up the *Holy Bible* of all slurs against women. It'll give me inspiration to keep on the re-write."

Interrupting what another person was trying to tell her had become a habit for Granny. Since Mildred didn't get very far trying to persuade Granny not to apply for the position, she headed toward the mirror long before Granny had finished her argument.

A Search Committee for a preacher was formed by the Light of the Holy Ghost congregation and its chairman phoned Granny for an appointment. The chairman was an old duffer who always introduced himself by saying, "I'm Doctor Bean, a graduate of U.C.L.A." When he asked Granny to come to the church for an interview, she said, "Not in this life or the next one will I go to church for no interviews. The church is a place only for worship. It's the holy house of God." As an aside, she whispered to me, "If you play hard to get, they'll want you all the more." That bit of advice sank into me like an anchor searching for the bottom.

Doctor Bean liked her answer. "How right you are, Sister Todd. That's the way I was taught at U.C.L.A.," he said. "Can we come up to your place, then?"

"You can tell me first over the phone what you got in mind, Doctor Bean. I'm re-writing the Scriptures and haven't got the time of day to waste on frivolities."

Again, Bean liked her answer. Mainly, because he enjoyed being called Doctor. Later, we found out he had obtained the lofty title through a three-month correspondence course and a one-week attendance at a retreat. As a reward for his efforts and the money he paid for what was advertised as 'a most intensive experience,' he received a framed diploma labeled in big letters, Doctor of Divinity and Theological Inquiry, from the University of Church Light Ascendancy.

"I am most interested in your theosophical pursuits, Reverend Sister Todd," he explained. "We are in search of a full-time preacher. I am the author of *Homiletics for the Layman*, and Chairman of the Committee for Theolog...."

"I am not interested in any committees, Doctor Bean," Granny interrupted. "But what is Homiletics in Hades hell?"

Being slightly deaf, Doctor Bean didn't hear her clearly. "Excuse me, Sister, what did you say... about a bell? What?"

Granny recovered her composure and, disregarding his question, said, "I might be interested in preaching again. It would give me a chance to try out my interpretation of Creation, especially with a theologue like yourself, Doctor Bean."

In spite of her earlier reluctance to meet with the four members of the search committee, it was agreed that they would pay her a short visit at our trailer. At the appointed hour, when the delegation came to our crowded quarters, Sister Todd was ready for it. She was dressed in a white flowing robe and a tall purple and red hat that looked like one worn by cardinals and popes at the Vatican, and she held an oak staff, roughly carved and nearly twice her height, which she had purchased at a garage sale on an Indian reservation. It gave her that extra touch of divinity.

For a fleeting moment I thought God must look like her. It was downright spooky, what with the beams from a lamp behind her sending flashes of light all around her head like in a picture of an ancient saint's halo. "My God!" I managed to say.

Granny had draped a green velvet spread over a big sofa full of holes, recently acquired for one dollar by Mildred and Granny at a Salvation Army auction. In front of the camouflaged sofa, which she soon turned into a throne, Granny placed four enormous yellow pillows.

"This is where my visitors will sit and have to look up at me. You have to set the stage to favor your aims, Doll. Don't forget," she instructed me.

When the members of the committee knocked at the

door, Sister Todd, who had been peeking through a curtain as they trudged across the muddy path in front of the rusty trailer, rushed to sit on the sofa. She placed the staff by her side and waited for them to knock a second time. Then she yelled, "Ye who are seekers of the Truth, come in through the portal!"

I quietly sat by her feet while Phyllis's nasty black cat, Tata, settled in Granny's lap.

As the visiting group timidly stepped into the trailer, Sister Todd shut her eyes, stood up and lifted her arms, staff and all, pointing one finger toward the low ceiling, the staff hitting the roof of the trailer.

"Hearken onto me, oh children of Israel!" she intoned, almost singing. "Blessed are those who seek after Truth, for they shall be the Teachers in Heaven!"

For a tryout, the committee members asked her to give the Thanksgiving sermon that was to take place in three weeks. The church would be packed. Nobody wanted to miss a Thanksgiving sermon by a great revivalist who was re-writing the Scriptures ("bringing it up-to-date," they secretively whispered).

As the day approached, I noticed Granny was losing her temper more than usual, often cursing a purple streak. Suspecting that she was headed toward some kind of trouble, I hoped something amusing would happen to break up the usual and unbearable monotony of a Kansas summer. Granny spent long hours thinking about what she would say at the sermon, and I frequently accompanied her to the Topeka Public Library where she searched for the great quotes from antiquity.

On Thanksgiving morning, Doctor Bean picked us up in his shiny old black Packard Sedan, registering over two hundred thousand miles on the dusty roads of the Kansas and Oklahoma prairies.

As Grandmother approached the car, Doctor Bean said timidly, "Reverend Todd, if I may, before we journey to the church on this memorable occasion, I wonder if you...?"

He hesitated before opening the door of his vehicle.

"Well? What is it, Doctor Bean?" Granny snapped.

"I don't know," he went on shyly, "I don't know if I... I...."

"C'mon, Doctor!" She gave him a friendly but definite slap on the back that made him drop his cane and almost lose his precarious balance. "Don't be afraid to ask," she went on while I picked up his cane. "We theologues are buddies. C'mon, spit it out!"

"I was wondering if you... would give me the honor of... blessing this old car of mine, Sister."

Granny beamed at Doctor Bean like a cat might look at a mouse she's about to swallow. "Why, of course I will," she said, getting ready to open her *Bible*, while she leaned her body against the enormous oak staff.

We stood for the short ceremony as Granny haphazardly parted her *Bible* and focused her eyes on the first line that caught her attention. She lifted her right arm over the hood of the big car and read from the book she held in her left hand: "2 *Chronicles*, chapter 26, verse 4, says, 'And he did that which was right in the sight of the Lord...' It is right that our God-fearing Doctor Bean should ask to have his car blessed, and I am sure it's also right in the eyes of the Lord, as the good book says, so I do now bless it in the presence of all these witnesses, invoking God's grace upon it, asking the Almighty that this car may last on this earth at least as long as Doctor Bean, to serve him for His good purposes without failure nor mishap, nor any manner of stalling or stealing, for a Theologue Doctor without a car is like a wingless bird in search of a home."

Old Bean was pleased with the benediction. He gratefully gazed at Granny, and effusively thanked her, saying he only wished to have the opportunity in the future to please her as well.

Knowing she had him in her apron's pocket, she moved close to Doctor Bean and said to him coyly, "Well, Doctor Bean, I do have a favor to ask of you."

Bean looked completely dazed, flattered by her request, deeply moved by her benediction, his right hand petting the shiny car, proud that it had been so thoroughly blessed by such an exalted personage. "Oh, anything, Sister, anything!" he replied.

Sister Todd took a deep breath and said, while she lightly touched the shiny car, "I must confess to you, Doctor Bean, I've always wanted to drive one of these old

Packard vehicles. They look so elegant. Distinguished. Like you. I'd be much obliged if you'd let me get behind the wheel on the way to the church for our Thanksgiving meeting. I know the way."

Without a second's hesitation, Bean blurted back, "Of course, Sister, here's the key to the ignition."

Granny hadn't driven a car for at least a decade, but she got in the front seat like a trooper. Her apostolic hat, bumping against the door's top, slipped onto the seat, where she inadvertently sat on it. Gallantly, Doctor Bean offered to carry the large staff for her but, since it would not fit into the car, he held it out the window.

To my surprise, Granny drove off smoothly. Even Phyllis looked at her with admiration as she sat by the window in the back seat next to Mildred, who blurted out, "Now, be careful, Mother. Don't get a ticket."

While I wondered how Granny was going to manage the higher gears, Doctor Bean, bent on making conversation, asked, "Sister Todd, may I inquire about the theme of the sermon you have prepared for us?"

As it turned out, that line of questioning was a major mistake.

Granny flushed with delight, exuding an enthusiasm bordering on exultation. "I don't mind telling you," she said. "I'm preaching about how the old men of Israel wrote the *Bible* to make themselves powerful before all women. Since then, all the generations of preachers have been bamboozling us women all along, Doctor Bean, all along, long, long...." Her voice kept rising as she made a wide circle at an intersection, with tires screeching.

"Watch out, Sister!" said Doctor Bean, startled.

But she was speeding down the long stretch toward the church, accelerating each time she emphasized a word: "'Unto the woman,' God said, 'I will *greatly* multiply thy sorrow and thy conception; thy *desire* shall be to thy husband and he shall *rule* over thee.' You hear what those men *saddled* us with, Doctor Bean? I'll fix them!" she screamed, fully slamming her foot on the gas pedal as we approached the church, frantically waving one arm.

"Put the breaks on, Sister, for God's sake!" Doctor Bean screamed.

The car jumped the curb, shredding the neatly kept garden in front of the church, and sped by a few of the early arrivals who looked frightened as they scrambled toward safety.

"Stop the car!" Mildred yelled as she was bounced around in the back seat. "Ticket!" was all she could say after hitting the hard top.

But Sister Todd went on, "I'll expose those bastards, the way I did those peckers at the Post Office!"

The old Packard raced through the open door of the empty church, right up the middle aisle, bouncing left and right among the empty pews until it finally crashed to a halt against the pulpit, demolishing it.

An ambulance was called. The three of us in the back seat walked out of the wreck with only a few scratches and bruises. Mildred frantically examined her bruises, worried about marks on her face. Phyllis and I scrambled out of the wrecked car, aching but uninjured, cursing magnificently. Bleeding, Granny managed to crawl out of the wreck with help and propped herself up by grabbing what remained of the pulpit. She lay on top of it and in a quivering but vibrant voice, she managed to say before she passed out, "Hallelujah, brothers and sisters! Awomen!"

Doctor Bean and Granny were taken to the emergency department of Stormont Vail General Hospital. He lost one of his legs but lived to be a hundred, although he never drove again.

The oak staff was unscathed. It had, somehow, bounced around and had come to rest impaled in the crystal window that portrayed the second coming of Christ.

Granny was cited for driving recklessly without a license and endangering pedestrians. She survived the ordeal but never drove a car again. Nor was she ever invited back to preach. She underwent three operations in a period of one month and, after her medical needs were met, was transferred to what were, for her, the familiar surroundings of the intensive care unit at Topeka State Hospital.

7

Nothing went well during the two months Granny was hospitalized. I was undefended against my sister's venom. "Should I be so weak as to need a madwoman's protection this much?" I kept asking myself. Luckily, Topeka State Hospital was located only a couple of miles from the wheat fields where our trashy trailer was parked. I took every opportunity to bike over there with the pretext of visiting Granny, so I could be safe, away from Phyllis. I became a nuisance to the hospital attendants. I would have gladly taken up permanent residence there.

"Dolly-boy," Granny said when I visited her the third time, not saying much during my first two visits, except for mumbling something about Mesopotamia. "Nobody else cares what happens to me. Your mom has shown up only once, while this is your sixth visit, if I'm counting right. And Phyllis hasn't come at all."

"Mildred is busy with Alvin, and Phyllis is going steady with another uniform," I informed her. "I can ride over on a bike in just a few minutes." I didn't tell her I was protecting myself from my sister. I hadn't told anyone.

The following week the doctors let us take a long walk on the extensive grounds of the hospital, and we had coffee and doughnuts at the Quonset Hut, where many of the staff members mingled as well.

Granny pointed her doctor out to me. "See that short man smoking a big cigar in the faded old blue suit, without a tie?" she asked me.

When I looked in the direction she was indicating, the doctor smiled at me. It's like he knew we were talking about him. I wondered what he was up to when he stood and walked toward us.

"Don't be rattled, child," Granny reassured me. "Everything's copasetic with Doctor Targownikstein. He's a good one."

"Rjeverjent," he said, slightly bowing toward Granny and putting a hand on my shoulder. "Zow is zis fine younk man yourj grjantson?"

I could hardly understand his foreign accent.

"The one and the same, doctor," she answered. Her eyelids fluttered and I was surprised to see her acting so coy. The only other time I had seen her flirting was just before she wrecked the car. "Say hello to the doctor, Dicky."

"Hello, doctor," I mumbled, standing up.

The doctor put his hand out. He was a very strong man, with a firm grip, and he silently shook my hand several times, looking at me straight in the eyes. I felt like he was drilling a hole through my head. I began to understand why *they* were called shrinks.

"Yourj name is Rjicharjdt," he finally said to me, emphasizing each word separately. Now, that was a man who knew right away what to say to a boy my age, even though he held on to my hand too long.

"My name is Richard, yes," I repeated. It was like I was discovering my own real name, what with everybody calling me by whatever struck their fancy.

"You arje a goodt boy, comink to see yourj grjantmuter zow often."

Well, I thought, if he knew that I come here to avoid my sister maybe he wouldn't be so impressed.

To my surprise, Doctor Targownikstein befriended me. He was the most educated man I had talked to in my life, and he was the first foreigner I had met, but I was only in the eighth grade.

Following my visits with Granny, I'd drop in at the Quonset Hut and have a doughnut. Sometimes, the doctor would treat me. After a few of these encounters, and just before Granny was discharged, he asked me if I wanted a job after school or on weekends. He'd pay twice the going minimum wage of seventy-five cents an hour. He didn't have to ask me twice.

My main job was to feed and clean his dogs and their kennels at his farmhouse a few miles from the trailer. The doctor lived with one of the occupational therapist women from the hospital. He had several Dobermans, all of them too friendly. When I'd come into their kennels, they'd leap at me and lick my face. I had to carry a wet towel to wipe off the slobber while I did my chores.

I worked alone on Saturdays, left a slip of paper listing the hours I had put in and found my pay the following week on top of one of the doghouses. I was left on my honor and, though I felt like cheating him, I had the feeling that he'd find me out through some mysterious power he had. So I stuck to the straight and narrow path for a change.

A couple of months later, on a Saturday afternoon, the doctor showed up and worked alongside me. When he rolled up his sleeves I noticed a string of small numbers tattooed on his right forearm. Since I observed that he didn't take particular pains to hide the tattoo, I got up my nerve to ask him, "Doctor Tragowgniksteen, how did you get those numbers on your arm?" I wasn't sure I had pronounced his name right.

He paused for such a long time that I thought I had intruded and asked the wrong question. "Rjicharjdt," he finally said, "dturjink zee var, zee Nazi chermans put zees tattoo on my arjm in a prjison calledt Auschwitz."

I gaped, not knowing what to make of somebody being branded like cattle. Maybe he was kidding, handing me a lot of bull.

"How come they did that to you, Doctor?"

He picked his teeth for a while, turned around and

walked away a few steps to resume washing down one of the kennels. With his back turned toward me, he lifted his face once in a while to get glimpses of the sky and began talking as though he were by himself.

"Zey didn't like Jews, Rjicharjdt. My rjelichion is Jewish. Zey killedt millions of Jews." As he began talking, I pulled out one of the doughnuts from a bag he brought for us to share and started munching.

He told me he had been in prison for over four years. One of his jobs was to pick up the bodies of people who were gassed, carry them in wheelbarrows and dump them on a pile of bodies next to incinerators. He said he had been beaten and starved.

His having suffered so much at the hands of the Nazis, his being so good to my grandmother, giving her medicines to take home, meant nothing to me. His giving me double the salary that other boys received and feeding me doughnuts to boot, made me put on a front, pretending I cared. I felt indifferent hearing all his past troubles, just as I did at P. D.'s funeral.

When the doctor finished the kennel washing and had explained the story of his ordeal, he turned around just as I wiped sugar powder and bits of doughnut crumbs from my face. He lowered his eyes and the muscles around his mouth seemed to harden. "Let's finish ourj worjk," he said, going into another kennel. His eyes were humid and I couldn't tell whether there were tears there, or a few drops of water from the hose, or sweat. He never talked to me about his experiences again. Maybe I hadn't been attentive enough, but when something doesn't really interest me I get bored and don't pay much attention. I don't care much about the miseries of other people anyway.

When I got through my chores, the doctor took a long look at me and said, "We have been so abusedt it is harjdt forj us to feel sorrjy forj anyone."

Me, abused? How in hell did he know? I hadn't said anything to him about my life. I hadn't been tattooed, or been beaten, or starved, but deep down I felt he knew my past hadn't been like that of other kids.

But it was true—I had been left alone to fend for myself, with a damn bone for a pacifier stuck in my mouth for years to vent my frustration on, and no one caring for me. I did have a Goddamned, patricidal pyromaniac sister who had pinched the hell out of my ass before I could tell on her, and who might try to kill me as well; an uncaring woman-chaser for a father who used me as bait; a madwoman as my only protection; and an exhibitionist mother who cared only for herself. Not that I gave a damn about any of it, but some people like Doctor Targownikstein may call that the background of an abused person headed toward big trouble. But as far as I was concerned, I'd just as soon have nobody to care for me, zank you verjy moch.

The next Saturday, when we met at the kennels again I thought, What the hell, I'll tell him my deep secret and see what he says. I wanted to shake the feeling of inferiority when I compared myself with him. Not that I would trust him, but I wanted to tell him something that might impress him since he had tried to impress me with his concentration camp stories. So I told him what I had not revealed to anyone. I told him the story about the time my sister burnt matches in the cellar. Finally, I told him about how, on the very anniversary of the day when P. D. cut my sister's hair, the house was burned down while he was confined there during an illness, and that I was certain my sister had deliberately killed our father. It felt great telling him a story of my own emotional upheavals.

"Zank you forj trjustink me," the doctor said after I unraveled the whole account. That angered me, because I had spoken not out of trust but rather to show him up. He didn't seem impressed, poker-faced as he became when I started speaking. Maybe he had seen and heard of so many strange events in his life, especially working in a nut farm, that nothing impressed him any longer.

For a while he didn't look like he was going to say anything else, but I could almost see the wheels of his sharp brain turning, conjuring up some conclusion. I wasn't expecting the response he gave after my long account. Although I didn't let on, what came so decisively out of his mouth just about knocked me over.

"You make up many lies. You are a grjeat lyink boy, Rjicharjdt."

I was perplexed. "I swear I told you the truth, Doctor Targownikstein," I said, baffled by what he had just said, upset with him for doubting my story.

"You are a liarj, Rjicharjdt, andt you know it. But zis storjy about yourj sisterj and fatherj—P. D.—is not a lie." He looked at me even more intensely than he had up till then and put his index finger to his lips. "Ssshhhhh! You must neverj rjepeat zat stjory to anyvone. Neverj everj!" he whispered. "If you tell zis storjy to anyvone, it vill only get you in terrjible trjoubles."

Perhaps, I thought, I am talking to one of the most perceptive people in the world. The two of us could really talk to each other. I'd begin telling him something and he would immediately know the complete story. He, too, was apparently blessed—or cursed—like me, with the great gift of intuition.

I thought he was through after his admonition, but just before I left his place, the doctor called me over and said, "Rjicharjdt, all the memberjs of yourj family must suspect Phyllis did it. You arje not the only vone, but shhhh! Rjememberj vat I told you. Shhhhh, no talkingk. And if you don't know vat to say, shud up. You hearj? Shud up."

I rode my bike back to the trailer, confused. But there was a lighter touch to my ride, an almost giddy feeling of discovery. The best way I can explain it is that I was in awe of a force Doctor Targownikstein exuded, a command and certainty over his own beliefs and fate.

Because I admired him I also hated him, for I realized that he was the only person in my life who might be superior to me.

The doctor had the complete collection of Charles Atlas Body Building pamphlets, a method called *Dynamic Tension*, which helped build muscles without the aid of any equipment. He lent his manual to me and I started locking myself in my trailer room exercising like mad. Getting stronger helped me feel like I could protect myself, just in case Phyllis did something vicious to me. Still, I wasn't ready for what happened months later.

Phyllis sneaked into my room before I got there and lay hidden in the closet, waiting for me to return. After I took off most of my clothes and began doing push-ups, she came out of her hiding place and, before I realized what was happening, she grabbed my penis and wouldn't let go.

"Don't tell and I won't either, Dicky," she said, overexcited.

"I don't want you bossing me around with sex," I managed to say.

"This is not sex," she answered. "A woman can give a man a massage, and that's all it is, not sex." I wasn't convinced. Strong though she was, and grabbing me where I was most vulnerable, I nevertheless relied on Doctor Targownikstein's advice to fight back in tight situations only if I knew I could win. So with the self-confidence I had learned from the Charles Atlas pamphlets in the last few months, I suddenly popped her a left jab in her jaw. Surprised and stunned for a moment, she let go of me.

Fortunately the confrontation stopped when the door of the trailer open and we heard Mildred's voice. Phyllis scrambled out of my room, bumping into her. She was still panting.

"What were you two kids doing?" Mildred asked suspiciously.

When neither of us would answer, she went on, talking to Phyllis "Were you up to some dirty stuff in Dicky's room? Answer me, brat."

"Dicky was showing me how he follows the exercises of Charles Atlas," Phyllis answered, looking at me.

"I don't believe you, you're lying," Mildred went on. And then she turned to me, "Is that right, Dick?"

Flushed from the struggle, for a moment I didn't know what to say. Remembering Doctor Targownikstein's admonition to shut up, I answered, looking at her straight in the eye. "That's right, I said. I was showing her how the exercises should be done. That's all."

I had been rattled by the event. That afternoon, on my way back from the kennels, I glided downhill on a long stretch of road, one of the few alterations from the otherwise flat land everywhere in Topeka. I had gotten into the habit of putting my arms out while riding my bicycle at full speed, pretending I was flying but, unfortunately, a small stone on the road made me swerve and lose my balance. I was catapulted to the side of the road, sent rolling on the ground for a while, and was finally stopped by a large boulder.

The next time I went to Doctor Targownikstein's kennels, my left arm was in a sling. I had broken both bones of my forearm, near my wrist, which would make it impossible for me to turn the palm of my left hand up for the rest of my life, but it didn't restrict me in doing most anything I wanted, right-handed that I was. When Doctor T saw me and learned what had happened, he said, "Goot! Maybe zis will keep you out of any futurje warjs."

8

As fate would have it, a young Mexican-American, wearing his impeccable United States Navy uniform, came to the last of the Moonlight Revival meetings. He was shy and small in stature, with black hair standing out like the needles of a porcupine. Most of the time he smiled at everyone near him, without saying a word. His name was Juan Pablo Javier Vargas Merino de la Torre, related to the most successful furniture salesman in Topeka. He must have been a hero because he wore a bunch of medals on his chest.

The moment Phyllis saw that uniform with all the shiny medals, she was entranced beyond containment. She slanted her head to take a more accurate look, squinting her eyes, nearsighted as she was, to get the sparkling uniform in better focus. She turned around and scanned the entire congregation, probably checking the other girls to see if any of them were also zeroing in on the uniform.

Alvin contorted his body on the platform, lifting his arms to the skies. He clutched the Word in his hands, his voice rising and falling according to the emphasis he was trying to make.

"Give your heart to the sweet Jesus!" he pleaded. "Shoo the evil Satan out and let the sweet Jesus in!"

I could tell he was at his most desperate whenever he started calling Jesus sweet.

Fifteen newly reborn converts from the previous two meetings had been enlisted to go between the benches where people sat, attempting to talk the congregants into being saved: Have you let the Lord into your heart? Have you been saved, Brother? Have you been cleansed by the blood of the Lamb, Sister? Are you going to give your life for the dying Christ? Where will you spend Eternity?

The uniform was among the last rows, which were occupied by my family. When two of the volunteers and a preacher came by the row where Juan Pablo sat, Phyllis jumped out of her pew to see what he'd do. One of the volunteers came close to Juan Pablo, clutching a *Bible* in his hand, and asked in a half pleading, half challenging voice, "Brother, are you saved and going to Heaven?"

Juan Pablo lowered his head in contrition, but was unable to answer the question in the affirmative.

"We'll pray with you, Brother," one of the volunteers said, nearly in tears. "And *for* you, sailor," he added.

"We won't let the Devil drown a brave sailor in the stormy sea of life," another one intoned, shutting his eyes and turning his head toward the ceiling canvas of the meeting place, while he draped an arm over Juan Pablo's shoulder.

The preacher looked at Juan Pablo intently, lifting

his arm and placing his open hand over the young man's head while he shouted, "Oh, Lord, help free this young sailor's soul!"

The two volunteers began tugging on Juan Pablo. "We never know when our last day on earth will be," the first one intoned, "and if you're not saved before you die you will suffer in Hell for all Eternity."

"God is merciful and He can save you if you let Him. Now!" the second volunteer insisted, tugging all the harder on Juan Pablo's arm.

"Come to the altar and be saved!" the preacher shouted. "What's your name, son?" he asked.

Juan Pablo looked around bewildered, not knowing what to do. He mumbled his name in answer, but the tall preacher, with stern eyes that looked fixedly through thick glasses, couldn't quite understand him. "How's that, son?" he asked again.

"Juan Pablo," the sailor said louder. "Juan Pablo."

The preacher seemed to relish the name. He placed both hands on the young man's shoulder and, getting very close to his face, said, "Juan Pablo, Juaan Paablo, Juaaan Paaablo, can't you hear the Lord calling you? He wants you to stop sinning and save you for life eternal. Come with us to the altar and save your soul forever, Juaaaan Paaaablo!"

Similar scenes were being repeated in many different places among the congregants. In the midst of screams of repentance and promises of glory, a confusion of sounds added to the surrealistic quality of the happenings under the tent. People scrambled toward the stage where Alvin stood yelling encouraging words to the various groups, cajoling the reluctant ones to approach the altar.

"Come down here and meet your Lord Almighty," Alvin yelled, "and if the light should go out on us before dawn we shall wake up together in Paradise—oh joy of joys!—with the sweet Jesus and the Holy Father. Come, sinners of Satan, and turn into angels of the Lord!"

Next to Granny, Alvin was the best. He could turn words around and around until everybody listened and was inspired. I memorized his postures, his way of moving his head down against his chin when he wanted to convey the gravity of his sermon, the slight slumping of his shoulders to indicate the burden he would have to carry unless the listener followed his admonitions, the sparkle in his eyes when lifting his head as he exulted over meeting Christ in Heaven. He could also cry at the drop of a hat. Real tears poured like a faucet out of both his eyes, for which he used a large yellow handkerchief he'd flash out of his hip pocket to wipe his face and blow his nose. I tried, but not a single tear appeared.

Once I asked him, "How come you can cry any time you want, Alvin?"

"Oh, that's easy, Dicky," he said, winking. "Look, all you do is tighten the muscles of your mouth upward and the ones around your eyes downward." He grimaced as he spoke. "And your face turns into the saddest, most awful-looking prune. Then you say to yourself, 'I gotta think of something sad, maybe my dog being hit by a truck,' so, before you know it, the tears start popping out. It's a cinch."

Sure enough, he cried as he demonstrated, but the giggles overtook me every time I tried. Alvin was a great evangelist, but he could have been an even greater actor.

He told me that one of the most important traits of a good preacher was the ability to use silence and the capacity to sustain it as you kept looking over the audience. "Fix your gaze on the sinners, Dicky," he said, "and keep looking at them. That's when the words you've spoken sink in."

Half dragged by the three men, Juan Pablo took his first few steps toward the stage where a makeshift altar had been built, surrounded by low, padded benches for people to kneel on.

Phyllis saw the uniform moving down the aisle and immediately followed. By the time Juan Pablo reached the altar, Phyllis was right next to him, though she had to push her way among the three helpers, who weren't about to let go of the sailor. When he knelt, she knelt right next to him.

I saw Juan Pablo the next day. He came in a beat-up clunker to the trailer and asked for Phyllis. When I inquired of him how it felt to be saved, he shrugged his shoulders and, to my surprise said, "I let them take me to the altar because I didn't want to disappoint all those people, but I don't believe in their bullshit. I guess I haven't been saved, as they say, and probably never will. I've been too close to death to let their words scare me."

Phyllis devoted all her energies to Juan. He was discharged from the Navy a month later.

I had gotten used to thinking of Juan Pablo as 'The Uniform,' although I never referred to him that way in front of Phyllis. It was a letdown for me when he came to the trailer one day dressed as casually as any of the Mexicans in town—wearing jeans, a faded T-shirt and a worn out pair of tennis shoes.

I was busy looking at one of old P. D.'s girlie magazines spared from the flames when I heard Juan Pablo's polite inquiry, "Dick, will you please tell Phyllis I'm here?" When I went to the door, I was astounded by what I saw.

"My God, what happened?" I asked dumbfounded.

"What you mean?"

"You look so different."

"Oh? You noticed, eh? I shaved my mustache?"

"No, besides that," I muttered. Frankly, I hadn't even noticed he had had a mustache. "Where's the uniform?"

"Oh, that? I was honorably discharged a couple of days ago. Civilian clothes are more comfortable," he observed.

"It's gonna shock the hell outta Phyllis," I ventured.

"She'll get used to it."

I didn't know he had it in him to be so cocky.

I really wanted to see Phyllis's reaction. I went to her room and said, "Juan Pablo is waiting for you, Phyl." I said it twice to make sure she'd heard me because she hardly ever answered me and this time was no exception. Then I hurried back to where Juan Pablo stood smoking a cigarette, waiting. He seemed relaxed, like he was enjoying himself.

If I had been shocked at seeing Juan Pablo without his uniform, what took place when Phyllis saw him was unbelievable. She came right up to me, passed by him, and said, "Dink, you said Juan Pablo's waiting for me?"

"Yes, here I am, honey!" Juan Pablo said, amused. "Don't you know me without my mustache?"

Phyllis suddenly took a wild-eyed look at Juan Pablo, her hands rushing up to cover her eyes, completely at a loss for words. "Ohhhhhh," was all she could utter at first.

"Mustache? Mustache?" she asked, after a moment of confusion. Then she recovered. "The uniform, where's the beautiful uniform and the medals? You know, the Navy uniform?" It was as if she was meeting him for the first time and not liking at all what she saw.

Never mind that Juan Pablo had received the Purple Heart for getting wounded in Guadalcanal; disregard the fact that he had medals for risking his life to save some of his fellow sailors in the heaving waters of the Pacific after they were torpedoed. Now that he was no longer in uniform, the whole community treated him with the same indifference, if not disdain, with which Phyllis now regarded him. He had a hard time getting any kind of a job in Topeka because he looked so much like a descendant of Montezuma, the last Aztec emperor of Mexico.

Without his uniform, and unable to get a job, Juan Pablo's relationship with Phyllis nearly collapsed. Soon after he was turned down for a job as a limousine driver for a large company, I heard Phyllis give him an ultimatum, "Get a job soon where you'll wear a uniform, any uniform, or else."

When he failed to get a job at the local banks where the guards wore uniforms, he applied for other positions that might provide one. But no dice, he was turned down by everyone, getting nothing but lame excuses, though he knew it was due to prejudice.

"Try for the milkman's job," Phyllis suggested.

He called the Veterans Administration and his old Navy commander and asked for help, exerting Kevorkian efforts to apply for the milk delivery job that would have gained him a nice white uniform. But there were five other candidates, all with faces as pale as the milk and cheese they were to deliver. He was a good driver and had much experience as a Navy Commander's chauffeur after he had been wounded, and was almost sure such experience would get him the job of driving the milk truck, but he was rejected again.

Disconsolate, he was at his wit's end, worried Phyllis would soon have nothing more to do with him, when

someone told him there were a few openings at the local
U.S. Post Office. A few weeks later, Juan Pablo showed
up at the trailer wearing the neat uniform Phyllis wanted
so badly. I had to agree with Phyllis that it really did
something for him. He looked taller, more handsome,
and the permanent smile on his face didn't seem as silly.
When she saw him Phyllis was delighted, throwing her
arms around his neck and giving him a long kiss. I had
never seen her so happy.

Granny and I watched the idyllic moment from a
small window. By this time, I was as tall as she was and it
was hard for both of us to peek out that window at the
same time. She shoved me aside, saying, "Man alive! Do
you see what I see?"

"It's just Phyllis and Juan Pablo, Granny," I said.
"He probably got that job with the Po...." I interrupted
myself, for Granny's expression began to take on that
blank appearance I had seen when I used to visit her at
Topeka State Hospital.

"You know I'm not supposed to have anything to do
with the damn Post Office, Dicky. Doctor Targownikstein's orders!" She hit the low ceiling of the trailer as
Phyllis was about to invite Juan Pablo inside. Within a
minute Granny was fit to be tied. I called Doctor Targownikstein and informed him of what was happening.
He told me to bring in Granny immediately for a talk.
"Zis ees an emerjchency! Come rjight now!" he yelled in
my ear.

Granny and I left through the back door to avoid an encounter with the two lovers.

When we showed up at the outpatient clinic for the appointment, Doctor Targownikstein said in no uncertain terms that Granny should never see Juan Pablo in his uniform, to stay away from him entirely.

Granny and I didn't attend Phyllis's civil matrimony two months later and, following doctor's orders, never visited them in their new apartment downtown just to be sure nothing dreadful would happen. I stayed away from them also and was relieved that I had an excuse not to have anything to do with Phyllis. The murderer—as I thought of her—was out of my life!

A year later, they had a baby girl. And a couple of months afterwards I heard that Juan Pablo was transferred to another city. I didn't even want to know where they went. Good riddance!

Granny, Mildred and I lived together undisturbed after Phyllis left. They let me do most anything and, in return, I protected Granny from the Feds. No postman ever dared step near our property.

Mildred hardly noticed Phyllis's absence, but one day I heard her mutter, "She made her bed with that half-breed and I wish her luck!" That was the last time Mildred mentioned her stepdaughter.

9

Time passed more quickly after Phyllis left. I was happy beginning high school, especially since the girls there thought I was handsome. I began to imitate my mother and spent more time in front of the mirror admiring myself, and when no one was around, sometimes naked. I could make myself look like a beautiful girl if I tucked away my private parts between my thighs. It was something I did to amuse myself and stimulate fantasies. I mistrusted girls and wouldn't want to give them the satisfaction of having me as their boyfriend to boss around, so I stayed away from them. The closest I got to girls was in my daydreams during my repeated masturbating binges in the secrecy of my bedroom.

I gave my first sermon on the date of my sixteenth birthday. Granny helped me prepare for it. She often said to me, "What impresses folks a lot is when a preacher can rattle off Scripture by heart and, Doll, you got a great memory. You hardly study and yet you get the best grades in school."

It was true. I spent most of my leisure reading comic books and seldom picked up a schoolbook, not even before exams, and yet, when teachers asked me questions I was ready with the right answers. I believe I was smarter than any of my classmates, but truth not being one of my strong points, I will confess only here in my secret memoir, that I cheated often, and on several occasions was able to obtain the test questions a few days in advance of the exam.

What Granny said was correct: "The reason you do so well in school without lifting a finger is because of your memory. All you have to do is hear something once, even when you're not paying particular attention, and it sticks to you like a leech."

I was brought up with Granny teaching me the *Holy Bible*. I could recite by memory entire chapters, word for word. She told me that the three most important books of the *Bible* were *Psalms* and *Proverbs* in the *Old Testament*, and the *Book of Revelation* in the *New Testament*. They added up to eighty pages. Not much for me to memorize.

Granny taught me you can find words in the *Psalms* to soften the hearts of your most hardened listeners. Every line in *Proverbs* lends itself to at least a few sermons, so if you're ever stuck just open any page in *Proverbs* and you'll get unstuck. And the *Book of Revelation of St. John the Divine* you can always use to scare the living daylights out of people and get them down to the altar to be saved.

And don't forget to sprinkle everything with the words of Jesus.

So in my first sermon, as guest preacher at the Light of the Holy Ghost Church, I used all three books before the packed audience and quoted Jesus all along. And I didn't read from a single note though I waved the *Holy Bible* in my hands throughout the sermon. There wasn't a space available and people stood in the aisles. Some had to stand out of sight of the pulpit in corridors where loudspeakers were installed.

Granny helped me choose a verse from *Proverbs* more suitable for a youngster like myself and, finally, I let them have it with the abominations in *Revelation* to get half the audience on their knees, pleading for forgiveness and salvation. I had them in the back pocket of my jeans, everybody clamoring for the boy-preacher.

Mildred sang a toned-down version of "What a Friend We Have in Jesus," to everyone's delight. She didn't sing it exactly the way she did in front of the mirror, but her voice was as seductive as ever, eliciting a lot of deep breathing from the men watching her. Granny—with special permission and specific instruction from Doctor T ('Sit zere but keep yourj mouz shut!')—sat behind the pulpit, ready to whisper something to me just in case I slackened in my presentation. But I sailed through without extra help. I made several references to the famous Reverend Sister Elberta Todd—a private joke between Granny and me since I knew she didn't particularly like to be called Elberta. She sat beaming, bursting with pride, laughing when she heard me call her Elberta and enjoying the adulation she received from everyone.

Although Granny helped prepare my first sermon, the most advanced lesson on preaching came from the horse's mouth, Alvin, who also sat on the stage behind me, loudly exclaiming, "Amen, Brother" from time to time, to give me encouragement and whip up the crowd's enthusiasm. I didn't think he would attend because there wasn't going to be any pay for him, but he showed up at the last moment. Perhaps he wanted to suck up to Mildred and show her he did care for me, not realizing that it wouldn't matter to her one way or another, that she was beyond giving a damn about her progeny.

Alvin invited me out to lunch the week before my coming out. "I want to find out how you're preparing for your debut," he said to me. He took me to the most expensive restaurant in downtown Topeka, The Kansas Hotel.

"Dick, come help me walk the dog before we have lunch," he said, getting out of the car. While I put a leash on Candy's collar, Alvin took off the dog's diaper and tossed it on the back seat.

During our walk we had to shoo away two or three male dogs who excitedly came over to sniff Candy's bottom. "They won't even let her piss in peace," Alvin said, kicking at one of the hounds. But he laughed when he saw a big St. Bernard hot in pursuit of Candy's trail. "I've been looking for one like this huge one. Don't you think he would sire some great puppies, Dick?"

Without waiting for an answer, Alvin took the leash out of my hand and went toward the approaching mountain of fur on the busy street in front of The Kansas Hotel. Candy peed and the St. Bernard got more excited while Alvin urged them to get on with it. I was looking forward to the event and some men formed a circle around the two dogs. When the St. Bernard mounted Candy, Alvin started cheering and laughing uproariously. The two dogs bonded, totally fastened to each other in a frantic grip for a good ten minutes while the spectators, mainly male students from nearby Washburn College, increased in numbers. They egged the dogs on, tightly locking middle fingers with each other, a gesture that, according to popular lore, was intended to prevent the dogs from getting disconnected.

I realized Alvin was drunk even before he took out a flask from his hip pocket, lifted it before the copulating dogs as though wishing them good health, and gulped a couple of big swigs. Soon after, he drained the container, slurping the last few drops, and shook it with a big grin on his face to show me it was completely empty.

Once the show was over, we took Candy—panting and exhausted—back to the car and ambled on to the restaurant. By this time, Alvin's steps were wobbly and he was giggling. "Dicky, my boy," he said to me, "if you live to be a hundred years you're not likely to forget what I'm going to reveal to you. C'mon, let's have us some steaks!"

But first, he glided over to the bar and, winking at me, whispered, "You're not allowed in here, so wait for me at the restaurmant, I mean restaurant. I'll be out in a minute. I gotta fill up again since I ran out of gas, if you know what I mean. Eh, buddy?"

Alvin feigned a poke at my chin with his left fist and dug his right elbow against my ribs while he laughed. I admired him but also thought he was an idiot.

By the time he returned I was seated at one of the tables, eating a salad. As soon as he sat down, Alvin began his instructions on how to be a successful preacher.

"People are fickle," he said. "You have to entertain them, like going to the movies. They come to church because they're bored. You don't want to see a boring movie, do you? And an interesting title might get them to go. My best titles have been 'In the Arms of Jezebel' and 'The Demon Inside Us.' A preacher has to look out for every detail, boy. The title is the first step into the church. Suppose you go to a home for a visit and the first thing happening to you after you come in is you trip on a night pot full of piss. How would that make you feel? The first impression is the most important in setting the stage, the mood. Sermons are shows, don't forget that."

Alvin told me about a trick he used to gain stature in the eyes of his congregation: "When a problem comes up, slant it in such a way that it looks worse in the eyes of the congregation than it actually is; make it look like an emergency. Then, you solve it and it will appear like a larger feat than it was. Presto! You're Reverend Fixit from then on! And don't stay with any one church too long. They'll want you to perform miracles and that gets harder after a few months. The first six months are usually the honeymoon. So, after six months to a year, move to another church. Never sign a contract for longer than a year."

He talked through the whole meal as he consumed the large T-bone steak and baked potato.

"What you saw out there, Dicky, with those dogs," he said to me, still smiling, "is the t... tur true nature of man." On and on he talked without letting me get a word in edgewise. "Men, I said, not women. We men are nothing but a bunch of dogs, just like that St. Bernard you saw fu... fornicating around with that poor innocent Candy. You know what I'm talking about?" I listened quietly, drinking my coke.

As best as I could make out, the Reverend Alvin S. Grabbe believed that men were basically irreligious and perverted, feeling at their best when there were no rules to abide by. He said we were a bunch of irreverent rascals who'd just as soon chase skirts rather than do any work, or anything else for that matter.

His conviction was that the entire religious movement throughout history would not have survived had it not been for women. Men get too bored listening to preachers and have to be dragged to church because they'd rather spend the time at a tavern.

I remember him saying that if boys had their way they'd never show up in church. "Haven't you noticed how it's always the women who drag boys and men to church? Girls like to please Daddy, and preachers are daddies to all of them. Girls like to sing in the choir, recite biblical stories, be Daddy's best little girl...." Alvin went on, imitating a girl's voice. "Boys are sick and tired of their parents telling them what to do."

I wish I'd had a recording machine that day.

"You have to keep women down, you know, Dicky? The minute they think they're equal to men, that they're like us, why that's when they won't need religion anymore," he said, starting to sober up.

Alvin leaned toward me all of a sudden, looked around to see if anyone might overhear him and whispered, "I'm going to tell you the greatest secret on how to become a successful preacher, Dick. Tell the congregation what they need to hear—that no matter how corrupt, nasty, hypocritical and unchristian they have been, regardless of how much harm and pain they've caused, they can be forgiven. Redemption, my boy. They want to be redeemed. And you, their preacher, are the one dispensing that particular bonus, the treasure they grope for. God must love sinners. That's the carrot you must always extend to them, Dick, don't forget that. God will love you, no matter what a miserable wretch of a human derelict you are. Keep 'em going after that dangled carrot and you'll get 'em down to the altar on their miserable knees. They'll crawl and lick the floor; they'll plead and grovel. And they'll give you everything they've got!"

10

A bald, cadaverous man, dressed in a black suit and a red turtleneck sweater, appeared not long after my debut as a preacher. He wanted to talk to Mildred. Behind thick glasses, his darting brown eyes were deeply set in his large skull. He carried a violin case in one hand and a heavy *Bible* under his other arm.

When Granny opened the door, the man introduced himself, "My name is the Reverend Wesley Neighbour. I came all the way from Missouri to see the boy-preacher and his mother."

Granny wasn't impressed. "Well, step right in, Reverend, and take a load off your feet," she invited casually. She pointed at me and continued, "The boy-preacher is none other than this here Richard Dink right in front of you, Reverend."

He grabbed my hand and shook it effusively. Turning her face toward the back of the trailer, Granny roared, "Miiildred! Mildred! Someone's here to see ya!"

Mildred came into the room wearing shorts and a skimpy top, with plenty of midriff showing in between.

Her face was camouflaged with a heavier coat of makeup than usual. It was a scorching day in early fall and all we had by way of air conditioning was a medium-sized ventilator that whirled warm air around in the back of the trailer. When Mildred looked at him, Reverend Neighbour averted his eyes, acting like he didn't know where to look.

The man was so tall that when he extended both arms the violin case and the *Bible* touched the ceiling of the trailer. Shutting his eyes tightly, he said, "I wanted to meet the mother of this boy-preacher ever since we heard about him at our mission, and now that I see you I don't know what to say so, I'll play my violin."

Granny winked at me while the man, with his eyes still closed—to avoid looking at Mildred, I thought—played her favorite hymn, "What a Friend We Have in Jesus," a coincidence that left me perplexed. Unable to contain herself, she belted out the song as seductively as I ever heard her, causing Reverend Neighbour to wince from time to time.

"What a fine voice you have, Mrs. Dink," he blurted when he finished playing, putting the violin away.

"And you play wonderful," she answered, straightening her shorts. "What can I do for you, Reverend?" Mildred seemed grateful, for his playing enhanced her singing.

Once settled in the small living room, Reverend Neighbour reeled off his spiel, "I represent the Worldwide Alliance of Christian Obedience, ma'am. One of our scouts heard your son's sermon and said he was a better preacher than most of...."

Mildred could hardly sit through the long pronouncement. She kept fidgeting with the straps of her blouse, nearly undoing the knot that held the front and back together, crossing and re-crossing her bare legs, peering out the window while the Reverend talked. "That sounds very interesting," she interrupted the man, "but I am right busy just now trying out a new makeup kit. I'll tell you what, Reverend, talk to Sister Todd here, who's Dicky's grandmother and has been in charge of his preaching education ever since he was in diapers."

Before Reverend Neighbour could say anything, Mildred got up and, slinking away past him, added, "Whatever y'all decide is okey-dokey by me. Bye. Good t'meet ya."

I was to be billed as The Boy Preacher, assigned to one of the several churches that belonged to the Worldwide Alliance of Christian Obedience, which turned out to be a small organization headquartered in Mobile, Alabama, and which I thought of as WACO.

In the United States, WACO had one mission in the poorest part of West Virginia's Appalachian Mountains, a small church in upstate New York among farmers in the Adirondack region near Heighman College, and another one in a newly opened outpost on a remote Indian reservation in Washington State. Their worldwide claim was based on a missionary project started in Colombia, South

America, and a one-room church they began to support more recently in San Sebastián, a small village in Puerto Rico.

In return for my services, WACO was to pay for my upkeep and give me a four-year college scholarship with room and board. The deal was contingent on whether I passed the college entrance examinations after a course of study I was to undertake under Reverend Neighbour's guidance. In return, they would require my services in one of their missions for two years after my graduation from college.

Granny insisted on coming too, and the Reverend agreed to take her along, using my age as an excuse. I was to abandon my studies in Topeka High and leave right away with Reverend Neighbour for Appalachia.

Before leaving, Granny wanted to see Doctor Targownikstein. I had stopped working for him in preparation for my first sermon. I could have easily left without seeing him again.

"I am sorrjy to see you leave, Rjicharjdt," he said to me. "Vee verje beginnink to get somewherje in ourj Saturjday chats." He put one of his strong arms around my shoulder and added, "You must findt someone you can talk to the vay vee dit because you can still be helpedt."

His English seemed to be improving. I didn't understand what he meant about me needing help and soon put the thought aside.

After Doctor T gave Granny enough medications to

last for two years, we were ready to drive to Appalachia with the violin-playing preacher.

Since Mildred wasn't making any moves to come around to say goodbye to Granny and me, I approached her, neither wanting nor expecting anything from her, just out of curiosity. Mildred was in front of the mirror, as usual. When she saw me standing a few steps away from her—suitcase in hand, ready to leave—she moved closer to me and finally looked at me, saying, "What you up to, lallygagging?"

"Nothing special. I'm leaving."

"No use moping about it. Bye," she answered, waving her hand and returning her gaze to the mirror.

Granny saw the brief exchange and got upset. "Haven't you got any sense in that pea brain of yours, sending away your only boy without as much as a hug?"

"I don't see you hugging me!" Mildred retorted.

"And I won't now unless you say goodbye proper to the boy."

Mildred came over reluctantly and pressed my face against her bosom without saying anything. If I recall correctly, that was about the fourth hug—if you want to call a brush a hug—I ever got from her, not that I gave a damn. As far as I was concerned she could stick her head in the oven.

Granny took Mildred by the hand and planted a big wet kiss on her cheek. "Now, you take good care of yourself, Mildred, and don't fall in love with that mirror," she said.

A while later, when we were seated in the car next to our driver, Reverend Neighbour, as the flat Topeka landscape faded in the distance, Granny said to me, "I'm sorry, Doll. Sorry I hatched for you such a fool for a mother."

This was, perhaps, what I would call the most tender moment in my entire life. But I had already put Mildred out of my mind and was thinking about the $215 I had saved working for Doctor T and the $320 I'd taken from the collection plates, all neatly hidden in my luggage under its bottom flap. I had my mind set on purchasing a secondhand car as soon as I could afford one and figured I was getting closer to my goal.

The trip to West Virginia was a big eye-opener. The tallest hill I had climbed was in the outskirts of Topeka, on the property of Alf Landon, the man Granny liked so much because he ran against Roosevelt for the presidency... and lost, of course. From the top of that hill I could see wheat fields going in all directions clear to the horizon on both sides of the meandering Kansas River.

Being a complete Jayhawker, my travels were limited to the state of Kansas, mainly around Topeka. I had never even been to Kansas City on the Missouri side. The only big city I had seen was Wichita, and it had left no particular impression on me, except it was the furthest West I'd ever been. Anything outside of Kansas was a big mystery to me.

I was glued to the window for most of the trip, trying to see everything. I could hardly contain myself when we crossed the Mississippi River in St. Louis. I felt enthusiasm, a feeling I had never really experienced until that moment, except perhaps when I tormented Phyllis's damned cat, or when I used to fry ants with matches when I was younger. Again, I marveled when we crossed the Ohio River in Louisville, while Granny slept soundly in the front seat. Although I could never get too involved with people, I was downright excited about the scenery. I guess the landscape was there to be enjoyed while people were for the most part an irksome bother. Reverend Neighbour kept humming religious songs and didn't register any emotion at the beauty of nature.

"I've driven through here a hundred times at least," he told me to excuse his apparent lack of interest.

Although I knew there were great mountains in our country from Geography lessons in school and pictures I had seen, I was beginning to think the whole country was mostly plains until we crossed into Kentucky. When we began to ascend the Appalachians of West Virginia, the Great Smoky Mountains, I stuck my head far out the window to see awesome drops into immense canyons that seemed to lead to the very bowels of the earth. Reverend Neighbour got worried. "Dick," he said, "you're going to fall out and I won't be able to deliver our youngest preacher in one piece. That wouldn't make me look so good."

I discovered then that the old fellow had a sense of humor.

One thing bothered me during our journey to West Virginia. I began having wet dreams where an attractive woman would fill my night visions. I'd see them taunting me seductively, touching me, saying openly sexual things I had never heard any woman utter in real life. I would usually wake up in a sweat with a puddle of semen in my pajamas. At first it was pleasant enough, but soon I got tired of needing something from another person, even if it was only a dream. For me, the dreams turned into nightmares.

A convention of preachers was taking place when we got to Appalachia, and since all six cottages of the mission's compound were occupied, we were put up in tents.

"That's alright," Granny said. "We're used to tents. Tents and trailers." She was laughing! I hadn't seen Granny laugh many times. Neither the hardships of the trip east, nor the inconveniences of the crowded conditions at the mission camp altered her good mood.

I poked her with my elbow and said, "Granny, you're in such good spirits since we left Topeka, I feel you've been born again during this trip." She laughed again. Twice in a row! "What's your explanation?"

"I've been thinking about that, Doll. I really have. And you know what I concluded?" she asked in a mystifying voice. Without letting me answer she said, "Topeka was full of pain for me. Aches. I sort of realized that all the more when I wrote Topeka backwards. Have you ever written Topeka backwards?"

"What do you mean, Granny? Backwards how?" I
began to worry she was turning weird on me again,
down the tubes for the umpteenth time, losing her hard-
earned marbles.

"Well, take the word 'Topeka' and write it backwards and see what you come up with and then maybe
you'll get my meaning."

I thought for a second then blurted out, "Akepot!
Akepot?"

"If you pronounce it a little different, it's 'achepot.'
You know, Topeka is like a pot full of pain for me. Aches.
In short, akepot!" she explained. Coming from someone
who had spent so many months inside a mental hospital,
what else could you expect? "I got out of the achepot!"
she kept saying.

The mountains, the fresh air, the change in scenery
were helping her more than the hospital. But I made sure
she took the medicines given to her by Doctor T.

11

If you think the farmers around Topeka are uneducated, back country hog raisers, you may be right, but they are enlightened wizards compared to the hillbillies of the Appalachian Mountains of West Virginia.

I confirmed an early notion I'd arrived at in my last year at Topeka: the more ignoramus a person is, the easier it is to get him or her down to the altar. No wonder preachers drift to regions where there's a plentiful supply of ignorance. The magical force moving us preachers, which we like to attribute to a mystical guidance by the Holy Spirit, is none other than the inordinate attraction that ignorance has upon our choice of congregation to lead—the dumber the sheep, the easier to herd them. In Appalachia, it was easy.

Every Sunday I travelled along the high ridges of the mountains and each time my destination was a different church between Bluefield, West Virginia, and Front Royal, Virginia. I delivered variations of the same sermon I had given in Topeka when the WACO scout discovered me. Reverend Neighbour and the other church leaders were enthusiastically pleased when they saw I was hitting the jackpot for them every Sunday!

Reverend Neighbour continued to drive us to the various villages. He'd ring a bell to wake us, and yell out, "Sister Todd! Sister Todd, let's get that boy ready! Let's go preach and save us some sinners!"

The first time we went to a church, I was surprised to see the big placard announcing me in large, colorful letters as The New Boy Preacher. Wherever we went, people wanted to look at me. They tried to touch me and were eager to pose with me while Granny took our photos with their cheap cameras. As the weeks went by, the announcement's dimensions increased, some spanning the entire street where the church stood. Often, there was a mob waiting to hear me. People lined up around the block and loudspeakers were installed for the overflow of congregants listening to my sermon on the street.

Some days I had to deliver a spiel at ten o'clock and then another one after lunch—a double feature. With two collections! Reverend Neighbour supervised all my sermons. After a few weeks, he let me do a few by myself and listened to my presentations while taking notes.

A couple of months later he said, "Richard, we should begin to concentrate on your delivery. I think you do well behind the pulpit and have the fire in your belly and the bones of a charismatic preacher, but the sermons need to be fleshed out with a little more grace and style. They are littered with clichés. More profound theologians would not let you preach in their churches after listening to you for five minutes. I also want you to learn to deliver a sermon, not only to the ignorant, but also to highly educated listeners."

I couldn't believe his counsel, feeling that I already was the greatest of preachers. "But Reverend," I protested, "I thought you liked my sermons."

"That's not the point, Richard. I do like your presentations, but we're talking about a higher level. We're talking about the exalted place, my boy. The place you might reach in the field of Theology, not just sermonizing. Don't misunderstand me, the Alliance administrators and I are happy with your work, but I, personally—as your academic advisor—think you could become really very special, one of the most unique, charismatic preachers."

"Reverend Wesley," I said to my mentor, striking to butter him up with a compromise between calling him by his first name and a more formal designation that didn't seem to suit our constantly being together. "Reverend Wesley, these people around here are, for the most part, like second graders. I hate to deliver sermons to them that they don't understand. Besides, all I know about preaching comes from my family plus another preacher who didn't have formal training either. They just picked up preaching and their language is the one I also use. Maybe it is full of clichés, but that's how we talk."

"Son, they may be poor and uneducated," he answered,

"but that's where the Lord's seed, planted by a boy, has no opposing ideologies except for the work of the Devil, so it's fertile ground for enlisting God's army. What you must do, Richard, is to aim your sermon to their level, and slowly help them to improve their ideas... and their vocabulary. Maybe it'll take years to make the transition, but we must begin to work on it. You are destined for higher things, my boy!"

He was quite sincere, a contrast with the hypocrites and flakes I imitated. I tried to clean my sermons for his benefit, but when I was sent to villages by myself, I let people have what would get them to come to the altar and leave a heftier bundle on the plates. Often I'd arrange things in such a way that I'd get to those plates and pick out a few of the five-dollar bills before the eager treasurers noticed. I figured that I was doing WACO a big favor, getting them all this dough, and it would only be fair to take a better salary than the twenty dollars a month pocket money the stingy sons of bitches doled out for me. I began to make fairly public offerings of my hard-earned but measly salary at special convocations when all those present were expected to contribute to the various WACO projects.

"Richard," Reverend Wesley gently admonished me. "We all know your pocket money is not substantial, certainly not enough for you to be so generous during these drives. Don't think for a moment we don't appreciate your offerings, but you need to take better care. You give more money than your earnings would indicate."

"Reverend Wesley," I said, trying to sound earnest, "you people provide for me room and board, clothes, transportation, my education, and pay for my grand-mother's expenses. What more do I need? My reward will come later, as we are told by Christ in *Revelation* 22:12, 'Behold, I come quickly; my reward is with me, to render to each man according to his work.'"

I had embarked on a purposeful project to train my-self to lie without flinching, looking at people straight in the eyes without blinking or averting my gaze, keeping my breathing steady, smiling confidently, no shade of hesitations, making sure my speech flowed evenly, never repeating words or stuttering. My body language was perfectly under my control. I made sure I always ap-peared open and relaxed, my movements and breathing flowing smoothly, never concealing my hands nor cross-ing my legs, a confident smile on my face. I could lie more convincingly now than ever before. Doctor Tar-gownikstein was the only one who had caught on but I never found out what gave me away to him. I did find out that if I quoted *Bible*, chapter and verse, with a straight face, looking right between the eyes of the dunce in front of me, it made lying easier. My biggest challenge was Reverend Wesley because he was the cleverest at WACO's headquarters.

Granny loved being on the road with me. There didn't seem to be a post office in sight, most being very small, often occupying no larger a space than a counter at a hardware or grocery store. None resembled the massive structures of city post offices.

Besides, Granny was much improved. She took to gardening and, saying she wanted to carry her own weight, became the cook's assistant, helping to make meals for the missionaries. After a few weeks, they put her on their payroll, earning minimum wage, eighty cents an hour. "Plus upkeep," they said, to sound less stingy.

Many of the visitors spent short vacations in the peaceful, spiritual retreats at the WACO campground. Not once, to my knowledge, did any of the visitors leave a tip for Granny.

Beside the six cottages filled with bedrooms, there was a central building of administration offices, with a kitchen, dining room for a hundred people, library, and recreation room. Neither playing of cards nor dancing were allowed, but they had a ping-pong table, shuffle-board, chessboard, jig-saw puzzles, dominoes, Parcheesi, backgammon, and a Chinese game called Go, played with a zillion marbles, that was brought by a visiting missionary from the Orient who referred to it as the greatest game in the world.

My duties were simple but they occupied me all day. Mornings were devoted to study—finishing high school courses so I could graduate and enter college. I was taught mainly through tapes and correspondence, al-though a teacher from a small Bible school in Charleston came every other week to give me special lessons and to test me. Afternoons were devoted to religious training and preparing sermons to be delivered each weekend, mostly under the guidance of Reverend Wesley.

The reverend enjoyed entertaining the hillbillies by playing local, twangy songs. After finishing one of their well-known regional pieces, he'd say to the crowd, "Now let me show you how your beautiful music would sound in a concert hall of the big cities." The audience loved it and looked at him in amazement as they heard the transformation of their music into a classical version improvised by the violinist.

Reverend Wesley Neighbour had studied Theology, acquiring a Th.D. degree at an eastern theological seminary, plus an advanced degree from Indiana University in the field of music composition. I was lucky to have Old Cadaver, as I was prone to think of him, for my mentor. However, I thought he was weak in his capacity to understand people. I certainly had an advantage over him in that area. As long as I could squeeze favors out of him to further my ambitions, it was convenient for me to accept the arrangement. But I was determined to drop him as soon as he stopped being useful to me.

Just after my seventeenth birthday, I passed all the courses with flying colors and got 98 on my New York State High School Equivalency Test, one of the most difficult in the country. I placed in the top two percent of high school graduates who took the New York State Regency

Higher Education Entrance Examination, competing with all those city sophisticates from the Big Apple. In the English section they gave me half an hour to compose an essay on any one of twenty topics. I chose "Can We Win the Peace?"

The results of the tests came a month later. All the sentences in my essay were interrogatory ones, a question mark at the end of each, an idea that occurred to me when I read the title. I didn't write a single declaratory sentence in the whole essay. It had been difficult to write, but I hoped to get attention if I wrote it that way. When I opened the letter from Albany, New York, with the results of the test, I saw that my essay had been selected as the best among all the applicants. I was ready for college.

12

For the first time in the seventeen years I had spent on or near Granny's lap, I had to separate from her. I wasn't worried at all about missing her. I was sure that once I left, I wouldn't feel any sadness or loss. If she had a relapse, they'd just take her to another loony bin. But she was getting along so well there didn't seem to be much risk. Granny was caught up in the daily chores at the campground, able to put some money aside from all the work she did for the mission, and she seemed well adjusted to life in that protected environment. Some of the older preachers remembered her name and her revivalist background and treated her with deference, which made her feel accepted and recognized.

A big convention of preachers, followed by a retreat, was to take place at the Alliance's campground in Appalachia by summer's end. Just before the event, the cook died in a traffic accident. Granny was the only one they could count on and she said, "If the main way I have to keep serving the Lord is by cooking for preachers and their families, that's what I'll do."

Knowing that the people working at the campground were in the middle of an emergency, I advised her, "Hold out for double of whatever they offer to pay you." She did so reluctantly but, sure enough, she got $1.60 an hour wages from then on. She was in seventh heaven. I didn't think she'd miss me.

The prospect of traveling alone to Heighman College in upstate New York, over eight hundred miles north, near the Canadian border, appealed to me. The trip would take two days by train from Charleston, West Virginia, where both Granny and Old Cadaver saw me off.

"Be careful when you change trains in New York City. It can be dangerous there—don't take up with any strangers, Richard," Old Cadaver advised. "Mr. Ernest Ernst will be waiting for you at the Plattsburgh Station when you get off there tomorrow. He will drive you to Heighman." He shoved a twenty dollar bill in my pocket, which I thought was pretty chintzy, but he was the most honest preacher I had ever met and that's saying a lot, seeing how I had known hundreds. Or maybe I just hadn't caught on to his game. After all, all his efforts were to lead me into the missionary field. His prestige increased when he brought in a new soul.

"My Dolly," Granny said to me at the station before the train departed, "you come visit me during vacations, you hear?" She slipped two twenties and two fives into my pocket.

During the year I was in Appalachia I had managed

to accumulate $665 by filching a ten or twenty now and then from the collection plates. A shudder went through me when I realized that the number 665 was just one short from the dreaded number of the beast described in *Revelation*. Better stay away as far as possible from that damned number 666, I thought! It's an abomination! But, of course, I shrugged at the thought, feeling superior to those who believe in stupid superstitions.

Anyway, with the $535 I brought from my savings in Kansas, I had $1,200, a stash hard to keep hidden. In fact, I had a total of $1,270 altogether with what I had just received, most of it hidden under the inside carton flap of my suitcase. When the train took off and we waved goodbye, I felt like the richest fellow in the world. I needed a car to accomplish my goals and now I could buy one, though I knew I'd have to postpone getting one for a year since the college didn't allow freshmen to have cars. I was also glad to get rid of these two people who were always telling me what to do and where and when and why to do it. Now I was a free man!

I arrived at Penn Station in the evening but my train to Plattsburgh wasn't scheduled to leave until just before dawn, so early that I didn't want to sleep in a hotel for fear of missing my ride. I checked my suitcase in a locker and wandered out to the streets, gaping at the tall Manhattan buildings. I stayed close to Penn Station, not wanting to get lost, overwhelmed by the largeness of everything around me.

Since I was hungry, I walked into a store a few blocks away called Kosher Delicatessen and told the lady who waited on me that I wanted a kosher sandwich (not knowing what kosher meant) but that I was on my way to college and couldn't spend too much.

She looked at me chuckling and said with an accent that reminded me of the way Doctor Targownikstein talked, "Zo, you hunkgrjy, mine boy?" I moved my head up and down and swallowed hard.

"Sidown, mine poorj boy. I fix a goot zangvich forj you dat you vill neverj fojgit. Kosher, he vants. Forty cents, OK?"

That sandwich was no sandwich, it was a banquet. She brought me many layers of meat and cheese packed in between pieces of rye bread, a mountainous salad with juicy pickles, steaming coffee and a huge piece of pie for dessert. It was the best meal I ever had.

I was on my way back to Penn Station when a woman approached me. She wore high heels, a tight skirt up to her thighs, and a loose blouse that barely covered her enormous breasts. Her face was covered with heavy make-up. Under her arm she carried a big black purse. I tried to move away from her toward the street, but she intercepted me. "Wait up," she said. "I ain't gonna hoit ya, fella. Wheah ya goin'?"

I kept walking away, cautiously, but slowed my pace. "I got to catch a train in the early morning," I mumbled.

"Well, in that case, ya got all night to spend with me." She indicated a run-down building across the street where a neon sign sporadically blinked its announcement, "HOT L" "HOT L" "HOT L," the missing E remaining in darkness.

"Oh, no, no, I can't stay. My train actually leaves in the middle of the night," I lied.

"Well, then, stay just a while. Ya won't be sorry, fella, I guarantee. Have ya ever been with a woman?"

I kept walking and now she joined me and walked by my side. "I'll give ya a frenching ya'll never foiget. For a young fella like you, I'll charge only five bucks."

I kept walking. "Sorry," I said to her, "but I'm on my way to a job in Pennsylvania."

She stopped and said, "I'll be right theah most of the night under the hotel sign, waiting for ya. Ya come back, OK? Ya don't even hafta come up to my pad. I can do ya behind the door. No one will see us and it'll take only five or ten minutes. Ya know what frenching is?"

I didn't know but nodded my head yes and walked faster.

"What's youse name!" She yelled at me.

I turned around, smiling. "Robert," I answered. I didn't want to trust her with my name. She waved her hand.

"Come see me latah!"

I shrugged my shoulders, resumed walking and turned the corner toward Penn Station.

I stretched out on a bench not far from the locker where I had placed my luggage. It took me a long time to fall asleep; visions of the prostitute kept coming back to me. I had a dream about her that would have turned into another wet one had I not awakened suddenly. I went to a water fountain for a drink and walked around the nearly deserted station, my feelings uprooted, struggling with impulses I had never experienced before. A big clock on a wall indicated it was one o'clock in the morning. I felt as though I was moving automatically, confused and unable to focus my attention on anything but the memory of the woman in the street. I decided to find her.

I went to the locker, opened the suitcase and put all the paper money I'd been carrying in my pockets on top of my clothes, except for one five-dollar bill, locked the case again, and walked out into the dark night.

She was there under the blinking hotel sign, puffing on a cigarette. When she saw me she pushed her chest out and smiled like someone claiming victory. "Good ta see ya again, Robert," she said. "Ya brung the dough?"

"You said five dollars," I managed to say.

"C'mon." She indicated the shadows under the staircase that led to the upper floor. "Theah's nothin' heah but them stoirs," she said to reassure me. "Nobody'll see us." She took Granny's five dollars and stuffed it into her purse.

As we moved toward the staircase I stopped and looked straight into her blue eyes. "I don't know what frenching is but I won't fornicate," I said, thinking about Alvin's bitch.

She laughed and exclaimed, "That's a good one!"

"Heah," she ordered once we were sheltered in the dark spot under the staircase, pulling her big, round breasts out of her bra. "Ya can play with dem boobs a while if ya want ta before I french ya."

I squeezed her breasts.

"You can lick 'em," she added with a pleading voice. "I like 'em sucked by a boy like ya and I'll give ya a real good frenching afterwoids."

I did as she asked and enjoyed it. She got excited and pulled down my trousers.

She was through with me in less than five minutes and I finally learned about frenching. I never thought a woman would do something like *that*. But it felt better than any of my wet dreams. Better than anything I had imagined. I liked the quickness with which she had satisfied me and the fact that I would probably never see her again. We didn't owe anything to each other and I could keep the memory of the pleasure she had given me without bothering with her. No need to reciprocate. I felt free.

I returned to the street as fast as I could while she followed me slowly. "C'mon back any time, ya heah'? I'm always in this hotel. If I'm not out ya ask upstoirs for me. Bye." She waived at me.

I was still feeling dazed, walking as though I were floating.

"Bye," I answered automatically. Then I snapped out of my reverie. It wasn't that I was anxious or worried; it seemed more like I had slowed down. I looked back at the woman and asked, "What's your name?"

"Friends call me Millie, but my real name is Mildred!"

13

The train hurtled down the tracks in the twilight of the early dawn while I sat absorbed in the lush scenery of the Hudson River and my own thoughts. Mildred and Mildred, I kept repeating, thinking about the whore and my mother while the clickity-clack of the train's wheels, like a singsong, repeated the name, Mil-dred, Mil-dred, clickity-clack, clickity-clack, clack, clack, clack, clack. Lost in the sound of the name, I was unable to snap out of this obsession. Not having slept much the previous night, rocked by the movement of the train, I finally drifted into sleep. Images of my mother singing in her husky voice, while dancing before the mirror, awakened me.

Awake, but keeping my eyes shut and enjoying the much needed rest, I heard the conductor's voice announce the train's mid-morning arrival in Plattsburgh, my final destination. The five-hour trip seemed so short I must have been profoundly asleep. I picked up a jacket I had used to cover my face while sleeping and reached up to the rack above to get my luggage. It wasn't there!

I looked around the rest of the racks on both sides of

the aisle, becoming confused as to where exactly I had placed it. But I was calm. I took a deep breath and searched again to no avail. I called the conductor and asked him where my luggage might be.

"Lot of people got off in Troy and some near Glenn Falls while you was asleep," he explained. "You was out like a light, man. God only knows who took your suitcase."

I gave a minute description of my luggage and its contents to the conductor, who jotted everything on a sheet of paper and had me sign it. I mentioned the $65 I had placed on top of my clothes, but I didn't say anything about the $1,290 neatly folded under the bottom flap. And now it was all gone. Years of effort. I hoped the bastard who robbed me would never pull that bottom flap out of place and discover the stash. I vaguely recalled a middle-aged man who had looked in my direction with some interest just before I fell asleep, the son-of-a-bitch. I hoped his hands would rot.

The conductor took my name and destination. "But I've seen too many of these disappear and never be found," he said, shaking his head.

They had already held the train a few minutes while we searched and there was nothing else I could do but get off, hanging on to my jacket, empty handed and totally broke, with fifty miserable cents in my pocket, goddamn it.

It was nearly noon in late August, ten days before

school was to start. I was the only passenger to set foot on the empty cement platform that sizzled under the scorching sun. The only thing I could think of was the loss of my fortune. But I told myself that it should serve as a good lesson from which I could profit in the long run, and vowed to be extra careful in the future, to trust no one. There went my hope to purchase a car, but I was determined not to feel sorry for myself, not to believe that it was a just punishment from "On High" for my misdeeds in gathering that wealth.

The minutes dragged tediously in the unbearable heat. I was thirsty and rushed into the station house through its narrow green door, searching for a drink of water to repair the abuses of the night, and hoping to find Mr. Ernst inside. But neither water nor Mr. Ernst was to be found. I felt abandoned in this calcified world of heat.

I took refuge in a shady spot under the eaves of the old three-storied green building and sat on a bench. The gentle breeze I longed for was absent. There was no one in sight and the road in the distance leading downhill toward the train station was empty. All I could see beyond the tracks was the forest and a tall sculpture on my side of the tracks, far away, with what looked like an eagle ready to take flight toward nearby Vermont.

After a short wait, which seemed like a lifetime, an old Studebaker, so dusty you could hardly tell its color, pulled to the side of the platform. I paid little attention at first because only two women and a boy about my age got out of the car. There was no sign of anyone remotely fitting Reverend Wesley's description of Mr. Ernst: a white-haired, jolly man of about sixty. The women were fanning themselves with magazines and the boy tagged behind. After the three had taken a few steps toward the train station building, I saw to my relief a white-haired, stooped old man get out of the car. He held onto a big black book that seemed to be part of the equipment carried by all the preachers I had ever met. The four of them walked hurriedly, like people who were late to an important meeting, trying to make up for lost time. When they saw me they began to run, waving their arms.

Mr. Ernst yelled, "Hallelujah! Praise the Lord! Hallelujah!" while he waved the hand that clasped the book. One of the women was very tall and thin. The older woman was in complete contrast to the first one: short and very heavy, with eyes that seemed to pop out of their orbits. She had a horrible limp and swayed from side to side as though a fierce wind was blowing on her. The only one who looked normal from that distance was the fellow my age.

Mr. Ernst was completely drenched in sweat. His pants were shiny and spots of dried food decorated the front of his suit. A crooked clip-on red bow tie completed his attire. He was using the *Bible* as a fan to refresh himself, and hauled out a rumpled handkerchief from his pocket to wipe the profuse sweat running down his unshaved face while shouting, "God is love. I *John* 4: 8!"

He grabbed me by the shoulder and stood before me. Lifting his hands—one holding the *Bible*, the other the handkerchief—he intoned with a grandiloquent and raspy inflection in his voice, "May the blessings of the Lord, Father of us all, be upon thee, and may the glorious light of His Son, the divine Christ, shine upon thee now and forever. Amen."

The rest of us repeated the word as in a choir.

Mr. Ernst began to laugh and went on in a distinctly different tone of voice. "My dear boy, we broke all the speed limits trying to get here on time, and we are still forty-five minutes late. I'm truly sorry. I hope you will forgive us." His face, with its stubble of white whiskers, was very close to mine. Spittle had accumulated at the corners of his lips. I tried in vain to avoid the nauseous stench which engulfed me every time he spoke. He continued talking, moving closer, disregarding my efforts to put a distance between us.

"Let me introduce myself. My name is Ernest Ernst, a bit repetitive, I know, but once you've heard those two names side by side you'll never forget them."

Mr. Ernst was like a rundown faucet that doesn't stop leaking. He kept on jabbering. "And let me present to you the reception committee I formed to receive you. This is Mrs. Laura Schmickel, the school's bursar." He indicated the senior woman. Very tentatively, she put out her hand. "And this," Mr. Ernst went on, indicating the tall woman without giving me any time to respond, "is Miss oh, I think Valentina Grankiokiviana, I mean Gradiskioki-viana, or is it Gra...?"

"It's Gradzkikiviana," she helped him out, slightly bending her knees toward me as she tried to look shorter with a vague semblance of an old-fashioned curtsy.

Mr. Ernst seemed relieved. "I got right the part about Valentina, didn't I? We call her Valy. There aren't many people with such long names."

Gradzkikiviana took a long look at Mr. Ernst and said, "I'm sick and tired of my stupid name, my Russian background. I'm changing my name as of right now!" She looked at me, her newest acquaintance, putting her hand out to shake mine. "My new name is Victoria Grass."

Mr. Ernst seemed surprised. "We've called you Valy for years."

"Never mind that, Mr. Ernst. From now on every-body can just call me Victoria, or Vicky for short. That's close enough to Valy. I do like it short, like my hair."

"I bless you and your new name, Victoria Grass, Vicky, for it says in Genesis 11:4, '...let us make us a name lest we be scattered abroad upon the face of the earth.' I'll give up Valentina Gradzikwhatever, and welcome Vicky, praise the Lord." Suddenly, he turned and said, "And this young fellow is another youth preacher like yourself, one from the Latin American jungles of Perú, from the city of Igui... Iqui.... How'd you pronounce it, Bob?"

"Iquitos. Iquitos," Bob said.

"Well, this is Roberto López, an easy name. Richard, just call him Bob. Shall I call you Dick? How'd you like to be called? Richard? Dicky? Dinky?"

Here we go again, I thought, feeling totally foolish hearing all this nonsense when I had just lost a fortune. "Richard is OK," I managed to mumble.

All of a sudden Mr. Ernst had an attack of laughter. He bent over and saliva drooled down the white stubs of hair on his chin. I could see he hadn't shaved in at least a week and, likely, not taken a shower either. He laughed and then he coughed, and then he laughed again, unable to stop. "Oh, goodness gracious," he finally exclaimed, taking a deep breath, "but don't you think it's funny, by golly? Don't you think that an Ernest Ernst meeting a Dicky Dink is funny?" He started laughing again and couldn't stop. But by that time all of them had joined in.

Just before we got into the car they noticed I had no suitcase with me. "Where's your luggage?" Mr. Ernst asked.

"The train personnel will get in touch with me if they find it. It got lost. But the Lord will provide," I answered, knowing that such an invocation was the way to finagle anything among preachers.

"Amen," they said as one, and immediately held hands to pray for the recovery of my suitcase.

Besides losing everything I had, the unnerving thing for me was that all the way to the village of Heighman, my welcoming committee talked about nothing else except how an Ernest Ernst had met a Dicky Dink.

14

I was privileged to be a star student preacher at Heighman College. To ensure I would flourish into a full-fledged missionary, the leaders of the institution—no doubt in cahoots with my mentor, the Reverend Wesley Neighbour, and his organization—carefully chose where I was to room during my first year. They picked the home of Mrs. Lucille Davies.

In the missionary field there was no greater figure in those days than Mrs. Davies. As a young woman at the turn of the century, she was riding on a train between New York and Philadelphia when she observed children spending pennies on candy. An idea—directly from Heaven—struck her between the eyes as she was praying in the train. Heaven's message on that particular day to Lucille had been short but very clear, "Pennies for missions instead of candy."

Lucille pondered the heavenly order and agreed wholeheartedly. "Children shouldn't waste their pennies on candy," she said. "They should give it to the missions instead."

Candy was bad for teeth, spoiled their appetites and fattened them.

She took up her new mandate with the World-Wide Alliance of Missions for God, which was another of Heighman College's sponsors, and an advertising campaign permeated the country. "Pennies for Missions" was so successful that several missionaries, including Lucille, were sent to Africa's teeming Gold Coast, where they turned black heathens into obedient Christians. Lucille married the Reverend Davies in neighboring Sierra Leone and labored in the 'fields of the Lord,' for forty years. Shortly after her husband died, Lucille came back to the States and retired in the village of Heighman. Now in her mid-eighties, she was considered the town's most honored citizen and no major event was taken seriously unless it was blessed by her approval and presence.

Mr. Ernst dropped me at her porch and took five minutes introducing me to her. He wound up his monologue by quoting *Bible*, "Dinky is still a stranger among us, so let's remember the words in Hebrews 13, second verse: 'Forget not to show love unto strangers for thereby some have entertained angels unawares.' So let's welcome this stranger among us. Welcome, Dinky."

There it was again, the hated name, Dinky. Granny had been right about how men just seemed to have a fascination for what they had—or didn't have—between their legs, for reasons they didn't even suspect. I winced and cursed him under my breath.

After Mr. Ernst's speech, it was Mrs. Davies's turn. She put her hands on my shoulders and quoted the apostle Paul's admonition to sinners: "Whatsoever a man soweth, that shall he also reap." For a second, her watery eyes so close to mine, I thought she was clairvoyant and could tell by just looking into my eyes about my adventure in New York, but I looked right back into her probing, light, oceanic blue eyes. "Let us get on our knees and pray," she said.

Mr. Ernst took out his wet handkerchief from his pocket, placed it on the veranda and knelt on it. I knelt next to Mrs. Davies while she held my hands tightly. Mr. Ernst and I didn't know when to get up since she continued kneeling. We finally realized that she couldn't stand and helped her up. "These bones of mine need to be oiled," she said.

Before Mr. Ernst left, he reminded me that they would pick me up later in the evening to attend the last of the village's summer revival meetings.

I was told I had the special privilege of rooming in Mrs. Davies's house over the requests of many other students who wished to get close to her for the prestige it would bring them. Some of them actually believed that being close to her took them a few steps closer to God's very own throne.

The mission supporting me paid her twenty dollars a month for the rent. My room was small but comfortable, with a window that looked out to the village's main street.

It had a cot, a chair and a writing desk, a bookcase, a floor lamp, a clothes closet, white curtains over Venetian blinds, and a picture on the wall of a handsome Jesus, knocking at a closed door, with rays of light falling on his face from above. Two other students lived on the same second floor where I stayed, each in a separate room furnished just like mine. Next to my room was the bathroom, shared by everyone living on that floor. Miss Lucille, as she was called, brought up to the rooms a change of bed linen each week. Our specific chores were to clean our rooms. She cleaned the bathroom every day and sprayed it with perfume while we were away at school, and told us repeatedly that she had learned humility while cleaning the bathrooms of the mission in Africa and by washing the feet of the black people. "Human ordure and dirt are just as foul as sin, and any trace of it must be wiped clean," she reminded us.

The two other fellows on my floor were also ministerial students. One we called "The Farmer Preacher," a boy from Western New York who nearly drove me crazy during my freshman year by playing the trombone at all hours. Miss Lucille was almost deaf and lived on the main floor, so she couldn't hear his practicing. When the rest of us asked him to quiet down, his answer usually was, "I'm playing for Jesus." With that answer we had to shut up.

Another wonder boy-preacher rented the third room. He was from Tennessee and was considered a genius, having acquired a reputation as a singer as well as a preacher.

Like me, he was barely seventeen, but he behaved with the arrogance of a frustrated old man, as though he should have the last word in everything. When I told him I was studying for the ministry he exclaimed, "Amen, brother! We shall make a fine preacher out of you yet." The condescending bastard.

I soon found out boy-preachers were not uncommon at Heighman College, and generally sponsored by congregations from different parts of the country. The place crawled with them, all very admired in their communities, each one hoping to sprout after graduation into a new Billy Sunday, the great revivalist of the early twentieth century. But that didn't faze me. I knew I could run circles around them.

The only student who impressed me was the one living in the basement of Miss Lucille's house. Chuck Wagner was four years older than me and had spent three years of his life in hospitals. "I was hit by a car when I was a baby and almost lost my arm," he told me. Several operations hadn't helped and the arm began to wither until it became a completely lifeless extension of his body, with fingers ridiculously looking like green beans. I had to restrain myself from laughing the first time I saw that miserable arm.

"We have something in common," I said to him, rolling up my sleeve and demonstrating my inability to extend the arm and turn the palm of my left hand up to a horizontal position.

"Well," he said, wistfully shaking his head. "I wish I had two arms like yours. Look at this piece of shit! What you have is no problem!"

In spite of the obvious suffering Chuck had endured for years, he retained a friendly, open smile. His father, a retired missionary from Alaska, was still preaching in Pennsylvania part-time. Although Mr. Wagner was the president of the Heighman Alumni Association, he had to beg the college authorities to admit his son into the college as a theological student because his high school grades had been unacceptable. Mr. Wagner received conditional approval for admission, but when Chuck registered, he declared his intention to study Business Administration instead of Theology.

It was during an English class that I discovered a kindred soul in Chuck when the professor, writing a long sentence on the blackboard, did so in such a way that her buttocks and breasts shook like a bowl of yummy Jell-O. I looked around to see if any of the other students had noticed, but no one seemed to be as struck by the spectacle as I was, except Chuck. When our eyes met, we smiled at each other.

After that incident, a relationship developed. He was the only one who called me Richard. I knew he'd come in handy—being a sophomore, he had a car. He drove and changed gears with his good arm and used the bum one to steady the wheel. I never saw a better and more confident driver in my life, even in the most treacherous, snow packed roads of the Adirondack Park's hinterlands. I developed, with certain misgivings, a kind of admiration for the "crip," as I thought of him.

Three days after my arrival in Heighman, a messenger from the railroad station returned my lost suitcase. I opened it eagerly behind closed doors and saw the $65 I had placed on top of my clothes. But when I unhinged the bottom flap, the big money I was hoping to recover was not there. The bastard who had robbed me had a $65 conscience, which is more than most thieves.

15

My reception committee came to take me to the evening's revival meeting. They were dressed up and, as they approached Miss Lucille's porch, belted out the famous battle-hymn of Protestantism, "Onward, Christian Soldiers." Leading them, Mr. Ernst waved his arms, holding on to his black book, yelling whenever there was a pause in the song. "That's the spirit!" Mr. Ernst put his arm around me, dragging me into the current of the procession up the hill, toward the outdoor tent they called the Summer Chapel.

The Peruvian boy, Bob, came over and shook my hand. He seemed so glad to see me and maybe said something about Incas being good friends, but I couldn't quite understand him, his English being so poor. He tagged along behind me.

Bob, a mixture of Spanish and Inca, had come from Perú a year earlier, sent by the missionaries of the World Holiness Church of the Amazon to finish high school, Heighman College's prep school. He was assigned to Vicky for English lessons. She had worked for ten years as a pastor's assistant at an Indian reservation in North Dakota and returned to Heighman to finish her degree, staying after graduation as a tutor. Roberto and Vicky were even stranger together than they were separately, he being so much younger and shorter, with a healthy bronze skin, black eyes and curly hair, while she looked washed-out, with straight hair of an undefined color tending toward brownish blonde. I thought he was a jerk for falling under her spell, and because, during his year under her tutelage, had not only forgotten most of his Spanish, but his English had progressed to only a few mispronounced words. Whatever he muttered sounded like poor Spanglish. How he was going to make it through school was a puzzle to me.

During the walk up the hill to the chapel I heard Vicky whisper in Bob's ear, "It's your last chance to get saved, Roberto. Go down to the altar and give your life to Jesus."

No one went *up* to the altar. Whether it was Kansas or New York, one went *down* to the altar, even if it was uphill.

Vicky pleaded with Bob in many different ways, urging him to surrender to Jesus while he kept saying, "Not *seguro*, not *seguro*, maybe, *quién sabe. Mañana?*" And when he hinted that he would think about it and maybe go to the altar during the next set of revival meetings, she said, "This might be your last chance, *tu ultimo oportunitad, Roberto.*" She liked to show off her scant knowledge of Spanish.

By the time we arrived at the chapel it was full of people and the service was about to begin. The members of the college faculty were seated next to the altar, where they had the best view of those seeking salvation, writing in their notebooks for reasons one could only surmise.

Three preachers stood on the podium. The first preacher lulled the audience into a state of sublime expectation and promise by singing in his well-trained baritone, "In the sweet bye and bye we shall meet in that beautiful shore." Then began the revving up enthusiasm with the hymn, "When the roll is called up yonder." Finally, to suspend all intellectual reasoning, he belted out and got his audience to join him with, "Give me that old time religion." At the end of the hymn he yelled to the crowd, "If it was good for the prophet Daniel... it's good enough for me!" He yelled harder, "And if it was good for your father..." The audience chanted back, "It's good enough for me!"

The second preacher took his turn inducing guilt by enumerating the wages of sin in the horrors of a Hell described in great detail, citing the punishments in *Matthew*. The third preacher went for the kill and pocketed the whole auditorium, so fierce and direct was his approach to show the way out of eternal damnation into everlasting salvation by offering redemption to those who are born again.

The third preacher was an accomplished actor. Looking at him I thought of my own presentations as utterly dull. After he finished his sermon, he said it was time to move on into God's saving grace. He extended his arm and pointed to the large crowd slowly moving from one end of the stage to the other. His piercing eyes transfixing the crowd. He let us have it, full blast. A sibilant sound came out of his mouth, first quietly like a snake ready to pounce but slowly becoming more audible until that prolonged sound pierced the ear and provoked a shudder in every listener, "Sssssssssssssss...."

I was perplexed, amazed at how much air he had stored in his lungs, and not knowing what was going to happen at the end of this farce. And then his voice finally erupted in a wild cry that was more like what one would expect to hear in the suffering bowels of Hell, "...Sssssssssinners!" he bellowed. "Sssssssssssssssssinners!" he repeated, rushing to the other end of the podium. "Sinners!" he yelled to the section in the middle. When he took a short run and dropped to his knees, sliding toward the end of the stage, people gasped for fear he was going to catapult himself onto the floor four feet below or fall on top of them. But he was able to stop at the very edge of the podium where he held up his arms and shouted with even greater force and conviction than before, "Sssinners! Be sssssssssaved! Get your redemption! Come to sssssssweet Jesusssss!" He had reached the quintessence of frenzy and his own apotheosis. People rushed in droves to the altar. Half the congregation was on its feet, ready to go down to be saved. I sat there between Mr. Ernst and Bob, amazed.

Soon, the main preacher was joined by half a dozen other preachers—including a few faculty members—who climbed onto the stage to yell out their personal version of salvation.

From the very beginning of the call to the altar Vicky urged Bob to join her. She kept pulling on his arm, saying, "Let's follow Paul and be missionaries in the jungles of Perú, give our lives to Jesus together. Come with me, let's be saved together."

When Mr. Ernst realized what was happening, he got up, knelt in front of Bob and grabbed one of his hands. "Oh, yes, oh Lord," he said in his most convincing intonation. "Help our brother Bob give his life to Thee."

"Amen. Amen," Vicky pitched in, standing up from the bench where we were sitting and trying to pull Bob to his feet. "Come," she urged, "come and be saved."

Bob kept staring straight ahead. All of a sudden he grabbed my arm, looked at me and blurted out a few incomprehensible sounds, one of which vaguely sounded like, "Dinky," but I wasn't sure. Mr. Ernst and Vicky kept pulling on him, determined to drag him to the altar, and Bob hung on firmly to my arm, pulling me. At first I thought he was afraid to give in to their demands, but I soon realized that he wanted me to accompany him to the altar. I stopped resisting and let him drag me. I'll never know if Bob really wished to follow his girlfriend's commands and wanted me to come along to protect him, or if his purpose was for me to be saved right alongside of him, unaware of how many times I already had been saved back in Kansas and Appalachia. Down the aisle we went, the four of us, Mr. Ernst screaming "Hallelujah," with increasing enthusiasm the closer we got to the altar. "He's coming, he's coming," yelled Vicky. "Oh, God, he's coming!"

As we slowly made our way to the altar, the congregation kept pouring in the same direction like an avalanche, all seeking redemption, which was the word everyone began to chant, "Redemption. Redemption. Redemption..."

We were filing by the section reserved for the college faculty when I heard one of the professors, a bearded man who had been trying to hear the words spoken by Bob, say excitedly to his colleagues, "No, that's not Spanish nor Incan he's talking, I know. He has been touched by the grace of God—chosen!—and... he's speaking in tongues!"

Mr. Ernst turned to me and proudly whispered in my ear, "That's the Reverend Doctor Francken, the college's Dean and professor of Theological Ethics, Linguistics, Creationism, Christian Evolution and Religious Anthropology. A great genius, ahead of his time."

I saw members of the faculty watching my group. I didn't want to give them the impression that I was reluctant to go to the altar, so I changed my stance and moved on my own steam so they'd notice my wish to be saved also. I embraced Bob and shouted loud enough so they'd hear me, "All I want to be washed by the blood of the Lamb, Hallelujah," and pretended to be pulling on Bob instead of the other way around. Several of the professors nodded approvingly while taking notes. Bob prostrated himself next to the podium, where several of the preachers were helping those who were kneeling, and he continued to scream out in tongues. Finally, Bob turned to us and burst out sobbing, "He talk about me! I ssssssinner, sinner, he know I bad. Oh, Jesus!" Both Vicky and Mr. Ernst were joyous at Bob's spiritual awakening.

When we reached the podium, I also started yelling my own confession and asking to be redeemed. Nothing would be better for my standing in the seminary than making a good first impression on a beaming faculty.

This is how, on my first day at Heighman College, I was born again for the umpteenth time.

16

The amount I received from WACO for pocket money was reduced by five dollars from what they used to give me every month while in Appalachia. They calculated to the last dime just exactly how much they should pay me by figuring the additional cost to them of paying for my education, which justified lowering my stipend. It made me angry, especially since they had earned thousands at the collection plates during my preaching. I was their star and they treated me like a hick from the prairie. Everyone in those hills wanted to hear the Boy Preacher. Now that their star was being sent to college, they paid me only slightly more than slave wages. At Heighman College, outside of the fifteen dollars a month, I didn't have an income.

Except for the occasional dollar bill that Granny sent me in her letters, nothing much jingled in my jeans. I began living a Spartan life until Mr. Ernst, witnessing my poverty, offered me a job. "Go therefore now, and work," he said to me. *Exodus* 5:8. He was in charge of the Heighman College print shop and was an accomplished printer, expert in typesetting at the Linotype machine, which could only be operated by hand. He put together the eight-page *Heighman College Weekly Student* publication in a couple of hours just before breakfast every Friday, so the edition would appear on campus like clockwork by mid-morning.

I am convinced that another matter influenced Mr. Ernst to offer me a job at the print shop. He had heard about my being a boy preacher in Kansas from Reverend Neighbour and asked me who had been my coach. So I told him about my grandmother, Sister Todd. As I spoke about her, he became increasingly interested, especially when I mentioned her aversion to Franklin Delano Roosevelt. When I spoke the former President's name, Mr. Ernst's face flushed and he became agitated.

"Oh, that miserable son of a so-and-so, forgive me Lord," he exclaimed. His reaction surprised me because he was so careful about not even coming close to using foul language, the "Devil's profanity," as he called it.

"You didn't like Roosevelt either? My grandmother was convinced Roosevelt had tried to poison the soul of the country."

Mr. Ernst laughed, slapping his thigh gleefully. "I used to pray for F.D.R.'s death and the Lord finally answered my prayer," he said in a hushed voice, gazing around to make sure no one else had heard him. He was delighted and that's when he offered me the job.

I started punching the time clock at the print shop,

earning the minimum wage set by the government at that time. On Friday mornings I had to begin at five o'clock to help Mr. Ernst with what a few cynical students called *The Weakly Stupid*. I was in charge of sweeping the place and cleaning used type. Every time a letter was used for print it had to be cleaned and placed back in the appropriate drawer. You really had to watch out for p's, q's, b's and d's during sorting, because they could get easily mixed up, especially if you looked at them upside down. It was a tedious job, but I could make ten dollars a week if I worked on Saturdays. Of course, there was no overtime, sick leave or vacation.

Mr. Ernst demanded my joining him in prayers during work. He insisted that both of us punch out just before getting on our knees to pray and punch back in before resuming work. At the least expected moment during a big job, he'd stop the printing machine and say, "Dinky, kiddo, punch out and let's get on our knees and pray to the Lord, blessed be His name." At no time were any of his prayers shorter than ten long minutes. Boring!

The bursar of the college, Mrs. Schmickel, one of the members of my reception committee, called me into her office one day. She was in charge of paying all checks. "I notice," she said to me, "that there are these holes of ten to fifteen minutes each in the punch cards you and Mr. Ernst submit."

"Oh," I said, "is there something wrong with that?"

"It's a little odd," she answered.

"Well, it's just that Mr. Ernst and I don't feel like we should be paid when we take time out to pray." That put an end to the inquiry and set me up as being a fastidiously honest chap, the kind of reputation I wanted to establish.

When I told Mr. Ernst about the incident, I gave it a different twist, hoping he'd abandon his habit of punching out during prayers. "Mr. Ernst," I began, "Mrs. Schmickel called me to her office and wondered why we have to punch out for such short periods of time that it takes us to pray. I think she was saying that it makes bookkeeping more difficult for her."

"What do you think we should do, Dicky?"

I pretended to be deep in thought. "I know what I would do, Mr. Ernst," I finally said to him. "I'd add up every week the moneys earned during the prayers and give them back to the Lord on the collection plate at church services." He went along with my suggestion. Of course, I never put any money on the collection plates. That's where I *take* money. I make motions with my hand, pretending I am depositing money on the tray just in case anyone is looking.

Eight hundred students attended Heighman College. The main building had a men's room with five standing urinals against the far wall and eight toilet bowls in two rows of four each, facing each other. Students and faculty had to walk between these two rows of toilets if they wanted to use the standing urinals. No separation existed anywhere in that bathroom so that one couldn't help but see the efforts students and faculty made in caring for their elementary needs. Some of the professors sat on their bowls, their pants and underwear scrunched up by their feet, correcting papers while they defecated. When the room was full, it was a ghastly sight, designed to turn an activity that should have been private into a public affair. Perhaps the school's administrators didn't want to provide a private place to anyone, lest they succumb to the sin of self-abuse.

P. D. would not have liked that arrangement.

Having to sit on the pot next to the exalted professor who just gave you an A, and in front of the reverend whose test in *Pentateuch* you took earlier in the day, watching them grimace and hearing them groan—most of the older faculty members suffering from chronic constipation—was definitely not my idea of how a divinity school should be run.

After I took my first course in Psychology I realized that the Alliance and Heighman College had a huge anal problem. In more understandable terms, they were stingy, holding on to every penny, having trouble letting go of even their own crap.

17

Heighman College was a co-educational, liberal arts school with an emphasis on Theology and Liturgical Music, founded at the beginning of the nineteenth century. Fundamentalist Protestant preachers wanted a safe place away from the world's temptations, where Christian students could study for the ministry. It became obvious to me that the founders had something else in mind—they wanted a religious environment for the matrimonial aims of their progeny. They didn't want to take any chances letting loose their boys and girls in search of mates. The preachers were fearful that in the wicked world, their children might fall for derelict souls to marry. Ignorant in the field of Genetics, they hoped a few generations of intermarried graduates would insure the propagation of the faith through ministerial genes, clones of themselves.

At ten o'clock each morning we were ordered to attend a half hour chapel when a few songs were sung, a short message delivered, and prayers and testimonials heard. Each student had an assigned seat in the auditorium, which served also as a chapel. Five absences could result in expulsion. Classes began with a short prayer. The college, approved by the Regency Board of Higher Education in the State of New York, also accepted qualified students who were of denominations other than fundamentalists. There were a few Catholic and Jewish students. These students also had to attend daily chapel, but they were not asked to pray. Most of them left after a year or two.

The college was located in the beautiful countryside south of the St. Lawrence River that marks the border with Canada. Small cities like Burlington and the capital of Vermont—Montpelier—were easily accessible. I hitch-hiked at the first opportunity, intent on opening a savings account at the bank offering the highest interest, to begin my new nest egg with what little I had made the first month working at the print shop and the few dollars sent to me by Granny, all of it amounting to less than twenty dollars. Instead of choosing a bank in a city in the United States, I went to Montreal, where I figured no one from Heighman would ever see me. Hardly worth the trouble of going there to hide such a small amount, but I wanted to check out the city anyway. I wasn't going to get caught with loose cash, no matter how small the amount. It was a good decision since soon after I opened the account I established valuable connections in that city.

There were no inns or motels in Heighman, only a hardware store next to the post office and a small restaurant that served as drug store and students' hangout. The restaurant was called The Green Mountain, whose most wicked product was coffee.

The village of Heighman grew around the college and there were no enterprises unrelated to its activities. Over three hundred of the students came from states outside of New York, and a few had been sent from missions in Africa and South America. Three quarters of the student body and faculty had grown up in preaching families.

People from Heighman were suspicious of anything that happened outside of their village. They, in turn, were perceived by neighboring villagers as odd and fanatical. The rules of conduct in the town were strict and enforced without mercy by the college authorities. Alcohol, dancing, gambling, smoking, playing cards, and even participating in the new love affair the country was having with television, were strictly forbidden. If you were caught kissing a girl, out you went, expelled from school. The faculty was even tougher on kids whose fathers were preachers, saying that those offspring were called upon to set a higher standard of conduct than children of other families. I had to watch my ass.

Singing or whistling of popular songs was frowned upon. Only gospel songs were approved. Banal talk, idle and unrelated to school activities, or the salvation of the spirit, was noted. If it continued, a message from the Dean of Students was sent to the offending student, with an order to appear at the office of an academic counselor.

Copies of such admonitions were usually mailed to the culprit's parents.

Bob and Vicky were caught *in flagrante delicto* in the Chemistry lab, which had a dark storage room that appeared safe, acting like a magnet to students with unbridled passions. Bob came to my room and tried to tell me his version. "She pull me to dark room in Chemistry lab," he said with tears in his eyes. "She want baby and to marry. Then we go mission in Perú."

I felt like laughing. Such an idiot. I told him he should go back to his country on his own and go to school there. "In any case," I ended my counsel, "you can't let somebody drag you through life, force you to do things against your will."

I don't know if he understood anything I said. Bob was a lost cause. It was one of the shortest acquaintances I ever had, with the least number of words exchanged. In some ways I wished all relationships were like that.

Mr. Ernst was crushed when he found out about the sexual activities of Bob and Vicky. He took a fifteen-minute break to pray for their souls. He ended up by saying, "It says in the first book of *Corinthians* not to have any company with fornicators, nor eat with them, to put them away for being wicked. The body is for the Lord, not for fornication. Give me the strength, oh, God, to put Bob and Vicky out of my heart and forget them forever, to follow thy command. Amen." After that, I never heard him mention them.

I found out a year later that Bob and Vicky had gotten married in Niagara Falls, and were living near Iquitos doing missionary work in villages on the Amazon River. When I went to tell the news to Mr. Ernst, he interrupted me. "I don't want to know anything about those two. I had a hard time trying to forget them. When she changed her name from Valy to Vicky she traded the Savior for Satan and that's the end of her."

Chuck Wagner, the fellow living in the basement, had said to me, "Bob and Vicky were stupid using that room in the Chem lab. There are a hundred other places where they wouldn't have been caught."

"Vicky wanted to get caught and expelled," I said. "She was in a hurry to hook Bob and get him to the jungle."

Although they were strictly forbidden, Chuck and I attended the movies on Saturday nights at the Plattsburgh Cinema. Admission was twenty-five cents. Being cooped up in Heighman during the winter months was an ordeal that a ride to Plattsburgh could almost cure. After the movie, we'd visit a tavern or go to a dance hall.

I managed to print at the shop a fake but official-looking ID card with my picture on it, issued by the State of Kansas, showing a date of birth that would allow me to be admitted into places where minors were kept out. When somebody questioned my age, saying I really didn't look like I was twenty-one, I'd say a childhood disease had stunted my growth and development. "He, too, had an accident," I'd add quickly, pointing to my friend Chuck, "and look what happened to his arm." It was a ploy that never failed. Chuck would show off that wretched arm with a jocular smile, startling the intruder into silence.

A few other students came to Plattsburgh now and then to participate in the worldly joys of moviegoers, bar hoppers and square dancers. We were all part of what we called "The Underground." There was an unspoken rule among members of this loosely structured club not to reveal the names of its members. The girls could only come to Plattsburgh during the day. Female students had to stay in dormitories provided by the college, while boys could rent rooms in the village of Heighman or at nearby farms. There were curfews for the girls, with meticulous rules for signing in and out. Using makeup and wearing short skirts or high heels was forbidden. Most seriously guarded was virginity.

On any evening of the week, at the Plattsburgh Cinema, you could count on seeing at least ten young men from Heighman College. Twenty men when they showed sexy movies.

Back in the village, many of the backsliders went to every revival meeting and got saved over and over again. Once I was asked by one of the profs why I was saved so often. "I am reaffirming my salvation," I answered, and no one ever bothered to ask me about it again.

Going to Plattsburgh risked a student's future. Being seen there by a professor or administrator of the college after 6 p.m. would cause you to be called into Doctor Francken's office the next day. And then you had to come up with a convincing explanation. The excuse had to be memorized and rehearsed by the student. One could not appear either surprised or untruthful. Straight answers were expected. If they could prove you had been at the movies, you could get expelled from the college and watch your past efforts and future plans go down the drain.

Plattsburgh was, is, and probably will remain what Granny used to call a "one dog town." But compared to Heighman, it was a metropolis. And there was plenty of sin going on there. Sin, not worth a plugged nickel, but sin indeed as defined by the theologians at the college, especially Professor Francken.

Members of The Underground had one hell of a good time just smoking a cigarette in Plattsburgh, making fun of the Heighman College rules. But once caught, you could kiss goodbye your scholarship, the years of effort, the hopes of becoming a great revivalist, and the possibility of getting rich. Old Francken would plant himself by the theater any day of the week—most often at around 10 p.m. when people were let out of the show—pen and notebook in hand, hoping to pounce on any unwary H. C. student.

I met the manager of the Plattsburgh Cinema, an old Hungarian, Mr. Mihály Vayda, and proposed a method whereby students were warned of the Dean's presence. A significant portion of Mr. Vayda's income depended on the tickets sold to students and he readily agreed. Whenever old Francken showed up near the theater, a small announcement appeared at the bottom of the screen for a few seconds, warning all members of The Underground, producing much laughter in the audience. The warning said, in caps, "BEWARE OF THE HEIGHMANIAC!"

Francken's morals prevented him from entering the theater, but he'd stand out there on a mound of ice for an hour during the winter, waiting like a buzzard to catch us. As Granny would say, "We showed the Prof he couldn't tie knots on our tails."

Of course, half the fun was in outsmarting the fool while we watched him from a safe distance as he hopped from foot to foot on the icy pavement outside the movie house, freezing his balls, with nothing to show for his efforts except catching a damn cold, which I prayed would end with incurable pneumonia.

Francken was the gatekeeper, deciding who could graduate and who could not. I had to take most of the inane courses he taught, like Comparative Christian Evolution and Anthropology, Science in Christian Doctrine, Missionary Ethics, and similar nonsense. Studying for his classes was completely odious to me. Outwitting him became a matter of survival, and a great game to boot.

Francken lived alone in an isolated old house in a ravine surrounded by a forest. It was a beautiful and comfortable home, with a couple of large, covered balconies that joined the house with the forest. Chuck and I made a careful study of the layout and became thoroughly acquainted with Francken's habits. One of his longest consecutive hours of absence was during his snooping excursions to the movie house in Plattsburgh.

One day when examinations were close, we saw Francken leave on his routine visit to Plattsburgh. While Chuck kept vigil, I climbed a tree whose branches led to one of Francken's balconies, and on into the house. Once inside, I found his study and copied the examination questions. One of the grandest satisfactions I got at Heighman College was getting straight A's from Prof. F.

18

Once each year, my mentor, Reverend Wesley Neighbour, was invited to Heighman College to give a violin concert. He used these occasions to counsel the students he had placed at the college. Appearing under the spotlights on the stage of the school's auditorium, he looked like a different person, so formally attired. I never thought I would see him in such elegant clothes. He was still completely dressed in black, but he bore no resemblance to his usual unassuming self.

Reverend Wesley was introduced by a fellow missionary who had just returned with him from Colombia, South America. "Reverend Wesley Neighbour discovered Indians who had never encountered Christianity in the Urabá jungle, near the Panamá border, one of the least explored areas in the world. He was warned about the horrors of the jungle, the danger of malaria, the foul swamps, the wild animals and untamed natives. We opposed his project of bringing the Word of God to the natives in that desolate area, fearing for his life. Disregarding everyone's advice, Doctor Wesley Neighbour walked into the jungle. When he didn't return for ten days," the missionary went on with his introduction, "we alerted the police. Most of us thought he was dead. But he reappeared a month later at the mission house in the city. At first, we didn't recognize him. His clothes, under an Indian blanket, were in tatters, his shoes replaced by a pair of straw sandals, his glasses broken over his nose. He still carried the violin and the *Bible*. But the biggest surprise was the presence of nine Indians who had guided him out of the jungle. I give you, ladies and gentlemen, the same man who brought nine souls out of the darkness to be baptized and take Jesus into their hearts, Doctor Wesley Neighbour."

Reverend Wesley stood during the longest standing ovation on record at H. C. He didn't like the adulation, shifting his eyes during the long-winded introduction, and began his concert, not even waiting for the applause to end. Though I was no expert, he sounded to me just as good as or better than the world-acclaimed virtuosos I had heard on the radio.

I basked in the glory of having him as my special advisor, and felt like I was being honored when my housemother, Miss Lucille, invited Reverend Wesley to her home for dinner and asked me to join them.

For Lucille to extend a dinner invitation to a student was an event that hadn't occurred since she had settled in the village. It was the first occasion I had been allowed to enter the downstairs part of the house. Several rugs and many African native objects filled the rooms, but what most attracted my attention, as well as Reverend Wesley's, was a series of small skulls on the mantelpiece over the fireplace.

"Sister Lucille," Old Cadaver addressed her, "may I inquire what these small skulls are? Not all small, I see," he added, pointing at a fairly large one at the far end of the mantelpiece.

Miss Lucille fingered the cuffs of her blouse for a moment and then came over to the two of us, giggling a high-pitched twitter. "That is my doggie, Max's, head," she explained. She moved the skull a bit so it would face us and picked up the next one, chortling. "And this is my little doggie, Maxi. Max and Maxi were among my best-behaved ones," she said. She moved on and pointed to the third of seven such skulls. "And this one, I present to you, is Frankie. He was one of my favorites. And here's my baby, Lily." On she went, naming each of her old mascots, and when she was through she blew a few kisses to them and continued to giggle.

"The biggest one," she pointed to the far end of the mantelpiece, "was the one I was closest to, although I tried, the Lord knows, not to play favorites. Dogs were my weakness, may the good Lord forgive me."

Miss Lucille told us how every time one of her dogs died she'd bury the animal, and on the first anniversary of its demise she would dig up the remains, break the skull away from the rest of the skeleton, boil it to get rid of the remaining bits of flesh, clean it with disinfectant and display it. "I still pray for all my African dogs," she concluded. She spent much of the evening relating anecdotes about the seven dogs that had been her faithful overseas companions.

I looked over to see how all this was setting with Reverend Wesley, but he was poker faced. I remained as impassive as he was, so he wouldn't notice my skepticism about Lucille's sanity. Old Cadaver truly remained as inscrutable as a tomb, and I thought that was a handy attribute I should imitate.

"I don't see that you have a dog now," was all he said to her.

"No," she answered emphatically, snickering, "I wouldn't want my African dogs to get jealous. It would be sinful to upset the little dears."

The following day I had my first formal meeting with Reverend Wesley. We met in one of the offices at the Heighman College Library. After we reviewed the classes I was taking, he wanted to know about my duties at the print shop.

"Most of what I do there is clean the place," I told him. "But Mr. Ernst has already taught me how to recognize and set up type, and how to store it properly. And I have learned to press single sheets and even format booklets."

"Good! I'm very glad you're taking your work at the print shop so seriously. I'll talk to Ernst about giving you some more responsibilities. We will need your printing knowledge in Colombia," he said, pleased.

He shut his eyes, wrinkled his face and looked up, maybe his way of getting in touch with The Creator, a gesture quite common among preachers. "Richard, there's one attribute in human affairs that's most important to get ahead in this modern world. Open your eyes to the one most influential feature in human endeavor that will move nations, my boy: Communication! That's where the power of the Lord will be used to bring the nations to His kingdom."

I paid close attention, for I knew I was getting the distilled experience and advice of a very astute and learned man. He went on, "We pass on our Lord's teachings with the printed word, with the spoken word, with images, with sounds, music being one of them. So, in practical terms, what does that mean?" He looked at me with piercing eyes as though expecting an answer.

When he realized I was stumped, he moved his face closer to mine, in a conspiratorial sort of way, and said in a hushed voice, "Radio, my boy, Radio. And now the new wave of communication—television." He tightened his lips and narrowed his eyes. I thought he could look into the very pit of my soul, but I wasn't worried. I was relaxed, my heart beating calmly as he stared at me. Then he blurted out his summary, "Printed matter, radio, television, and the right kind of motion pictures. Those four avenues will place the power of the world in the hands of Jesus!" He then put his hand on my knee and whispered to me, filling me with enthusiasm. "Maybe you, Richard. Maybe you will be our great minister of the airwaves. Let us bow our heads in prayer, son."

He prayed with tears in his eyes, asking God to help me find the way to use the tools of communication he had mentioned and which I was to remember well. "Our good Lord will show you the way. He always does, if you open your heart to Him," the Reverend said after he finished praying, eyes still closed, a beatific smile making him look like a starved saint.

"Reverend Wesley," I ventured to ask, "there are two matters I'd like your counsel on."

He looked at me inquisitively. "Well, tell me about them and we'll see what we can do."

"One of them is that I'm very curious about taking courses in psychology, maybe minoring in it. I think it might help me as a preacher, you know, figuring out the mind, and to make friends and influence people, like it says in that book everyone is reading lately."

"And the other?" he asked, nodding his head in agreement.

"Well," I hesitated, "it's about my staying at Sister Lucille's place next year. I have appreciated it but Chuck Wagner, a friend of mine—from a preacher's family also—and I thought we'd rent a small two-bedroom apartment."

"I can see it might be hard to listen to all her stories about dead dogs," he said, and consented to my two requests.

After reviewing the papers I had written, Reverend Wesley provided me with his recommendation of courses to take the following semester: New Testament, Biblical Greek, Life of Christ, Foreign Missions, Introduction to Psychology, and Spanish. "Well," he added, pleased with himself, "do you think you'll be ready to spend a summer with me in the jungles of Colombia after your sophomore year? You have to begin working to pay for the scholarship, and that will start you off. And then we'll convert us a bunch of natives."

19

I pondered the advice given to me by my mentor and noticed how both he and my previous adviser, the Reverend Alvin Grabbe, had been very mindful about Power, each one for different reasons and purposes. As far as I was concerned, they were both hypocrites.

Neither of them gave a hoot about improving the conditions of the rest of humanity. Not that I cared a damn about that either. But the immediacy and practicality of Alvin's teachings and example were more beguiling. Reverend Wesley Neighbour's entailed a life of self-abnegation and restraint impossible to follow unless you were a saint or a deluded fool. Although he was certainly committed to his faith, Reverend Wesley's overwhelming sanctimoniousness, and his whole lifestyle in general, made me sick. The Power I wanted was not to be shared with any gods.

At Heighman College, unless you kissed Dean Francken's ass, you were seriously handicapped. Dean Francken controlled all privileges. Upperclassmen—mostly seniors and a few juniors—could get assignments as interim preacher, to substitute for ministers absent in areas near the college, and be the recipients of invitations to preach in upstate New York, parts of New England, as well as the Canadian provinces of southern Ontario and Québec across the nearby St. Lawrence river.

One could make thirty to fifty dollars for a sermon, transportation expenses paid, including overnight stay and meals. Needless to say, much prestige was associated with being named interim preacher and one could begin extending one's influence by receiving such a privilege.

Following Alvin's advice to always be on the right side of the most influential person, I decided to direct my adulation to Dean Francken, hoping to be named interim preacher. Inadvertently, Mr. Ernst gave me the idea about how to do it. We were putting together the student paper one Friday morning when he said to me, "There's this column in the *Weekly* that deals with the Biblical command found in the book of *Ecclesiastes*, chapter 3, verses 1 and 2, where it says, 'For everything there is a season, and a time for every purpose under heaven: a time to be born and a time to die.' The student who started this column is graduating and, unfortunately, that will be the end of 'A Time to Be Born' unless you apply for the job."

"Do you think I could write the column, Mr. Ernst? The paper's editors don't favor sophomores, you know."

"Well, Dinky, that's up to the Lord. Let's get on our knees and ask Him. He will send you a sign."

For eleven minutes he prayed, invoking God's help to send us a sign. Every time he put on these prayer stints in my presence, I nearly died of boredom. My only source of distraction, which I knew he wouldn't object to, was to read a *Bible* while he prayed. At least I could get ready for a class assignment during his chat with the Lord. I looked up the citation in *Ecclesiastes* and found that a few lines further into the chapter cited, in verse 4, it read, "A time to weep, and a time to laugh."

When Mr. Ernst finished his prayer, I lifted my arms in the style he had taught me and said, "Amen, Mr. Ernst. A light just came into my spirit. It was the sign you were praying for."

"Blessed be the almighty Lord in heaven!" Mr. Ernst declaimed, beaming. "He answered so soon, hallelujah!"

"I will write the column, Mr. Ernst. I will write it as God Himself told me to. He said to call it 'A Time to Laugh!' "

"That's the next verse!" he yelled. Mr. Ernst was beside himself and embraced me. "A time to laugh?" he said. "How marvelous."

I had learned to deal with his impulses to grab me at the least expected moment and embrace me while he revealed some intimate detail about his relationship to the Almighty or the account of what he called a miracle. To be on the safe side, however, I held my breath while he hugged me.

I then presented three samples of my proposal to

the editor. One of these samples was an article about the joviality and gracious humor, the ability to make people feel good and laugh, and whatever qualities I invented about Dean Francken and his selfless way of sharing his wisdom. It was printed in the first issue of the following semester with a note saying that the outgoing column, "A Time to Be Born," was being substituted by "A Time to Laugh," citing, of course, the Biblical reference where both themes were taken. I followed my first article with two others about heads of departments, both professors high in the academic pyramid of the college. A few weeks later I received a congratulatory letter saying that I had been unanimously selected as the first sophomore to be placed on the select list of interim preachers. The long-winded note, signed by Dean Francken and three of his cronies of the selection committee, stated that my first assignments would soon be forthcoming with payment of $45 for each appearance.

In my mind, I changed the name of my column from "A Time to Laugh" to "A Time to Kiss Ass." Of course, I had long abandoned going to the movies at Plattsburgh and having anything to do with The Underground for fear that some jealous soul might betray me and expose my hypocrisy, forcing me to find devious ways to dispose of him, without getting caught, of course.

My increase in income brought me in closer contact with Chuck. From the very beginning of his training in business administration, Chuck showed unusually astute financial savvy. Each of the students in his group had to present a mock portfolio of investments on a monthly basis. Chuck's portfolio was usually the top performer, showing his remarkable understanding and intuition about the stock market's gyrations. I kept his counsel in all matters regarding investments. As long as I was getting valuable instruction from Chuck, I figured it was worth keeping him around.

Chuck also excelled in sports. Anything that could be played without using the right arm interested him. He had an advantage playing soccer. "The fact that I have so short a right arm and practically no hand makes it easier for me to play international football because there's half the likelihood that I'll touch a ball with only one arm available," he explained grinning while he winked at me. "I'm less exposed."

Chuck played tennis, and by his senior year he had won the Intercollegiate Ministerial Alliance championship series against seven other theological schools.

With my advice, during the last moments of the championship game, Chuck flopped out of his pocket the warped appendage which glared in full view of the puzzled opponent, distracting him enough to lose his last serve, and the game. When Chuck was criticized, I came to his defense saying that he couldn't help it if he had a scary arm that came out of hiding when least expected.

Chuck invited me to spend spring vacation with him at his home in Bradford, Pennsylvania, just across the line of the southwestern New York State border. It was a long ride through the length of the state. I had never seen such enormous barns as I saw during that trip, made all the more fun for me since Chuck was teaching me how to drive, even though I didn't have a learner's permit. I was determined to purchase a car as soon as possible.

Along the way, the theme of girls was raised. He seemed to have vast experience with them. I was secretive by nature and well acquainted with the arithmetic of secrecy. In my accounting book, you only told a secret if you were made privy to a more revealing one first.

In Bradford, Chuck said to me, "There are a couple of whorehouses we can visit where the women will do anything for five dollars, anything. I've been there and, believe me, what those women do to you will kink your hair." Still, I refrained from bragging about my adventure with the prostitute in New York.

I had saved fifteen dollars for the trip. After I paid my share of the gas expenses from Heighman to Bradford and back, I scarcely had five dollars left. I needed money if we were going to one of Bradford's pleasure dens.

An opportunity to get a few loose dollars presented itself when Chuck's father, Reverend Wagner, asked me if I'd collect the money solicited at the next Sunday school. The regular custodian of the plate was away and Reverend Wagner wanted to keep me occupied while Chuck was busy doing some other church-related chore.

In looking over the records of the donations made in months passed, I saw that the minimum was $349, and the maximum $498. Thanksgiving was the day when the donations were highest, followed by Easter Sunday, when $470 had been collected the previous year. Christmas rated a low third, with $426 coming in. People spent most of their money on gifts.

After I collected the donations, adding up all the money to make my report, I realized with much satisfaction that $530.12 had been left on the plates. When I handed in $500.12, both the treasurer and Reverend Wagner beamed with delight. "We've never had such a generous donation during Easter. The Lord is good to us," he said.

20

When Reverend Wesley Neighbour approved the Spanish course as one of my subjects, he said, "It will help your communication skills with the natives next summer in South America."

I feared I would receive a mediocre grade in that language, which would wreck the nearly perfect average I had, but there was no way I could get into the professor's house and copy the test's questions, what with the eminent schoolmarm from Spain living together with three other spinster faculty members in a house next to the campus. Besides, the Spanish professor graded on the basis of weekly short quizzes.

I met a student in class who spoke Spanish fluently and wanted to boost his sagging grade point average with an A. His name was Jesús Lehman, the son of American missionaries in Costa Rica. He sat next to me and we arranged for him to write his answers in large letters that I could easily copy. I got a B+ and the teacher was grateful for the big letters in Jesús's test answers since her myopia made it difficult for her to read normal writing.

One day after class, Jesús approached me with a deal I couldn't pass up. "My parents have a business arrangement with a publisher in Alabama," he said to me, "and this outfit sent me a hundred cross-referenced *Bibles* and a hundred encyclopedias." He pulled out of a bag two huge, colorfully illustrated, hardbound volumes with flashy, gilt-edged pages. One was a *Bible*, the other, an encyclopedia. They were gaudy presentations.

"On Saturdays, we could sell these books," he went on, showing me the price list on a sheet of paper in the Alabama publisher's letterhead. The proposal was to sell each volume for fifty dollars and keep ten percent as commission. The publisher and his parents' mission in Costa Rica would share the profit. "You can sell on one street and I'll try another one. We can start selling in Plattsburgh next Saturday morning."

"And what about our commission, how do we deal with that?" I wanted to know.

"Simple. Any book we sell will get us a ten-dollar commission."

"What if you sell five and I don't sell any?" I wanted to make the deal more specific so there would be no mix-up later.

"If I sell five, I get fifty dollars, and you get zip. Nothing," he laughed.

I turned out to be a pretty good salesman, testifying for sweet Jesus first, then letting them know that the proceeds would be sent to a Christian mission in Costa

Rica. I sold seven *Bibles* and two encyclopedias when we worked over the good people of Plattsburgh the following Saturday, knocking at the doors of one of its nicest neighborhoods for eight hours straight.

We met by Jesús's car in the late afternoon, and, like a damn fool, I handed over the $450 I had received for my day's work. His face turned pale. I thought he was going to faint. He started stuttering and blinking. He could hardly contain himself. "Mmmmy Gogogod, how in the woworld you sold so mmmany?" I had never heard him stutter before.

"Simple," I said. "I sold seven *Bibles* and two encyclopedias, a total of nine books."

His long silence told me the news didn't settle well with him. "Well?" I inquired, dying of curiosity. "And how did you make out?"

He blinked more rapidly, shook his head and said nothing for a long while. Finally, he mumbled almost inaudibly, "I only sold two damn *Bibles*. The entire day. I can't believe it." He lowered his voice, "and not a single encyclopedia."

"The encyclopedias are harder to sell, Jesús." I tried to cheer him up and get my commission. "Next time, you'll do better. Still, you made twenty dollars, man. I'll take my ninety now." I put my hand out, waiting for him to return my share.

"We have to wait to get our commissions until the publisher sends us the check."

What he said stunned me, but I said nothing. I didn't confront him with the statement he had made before we started, knowing it would be futile, realizing that I was dealing with a damn cheat.

Jesús stashed the bundle of dough in a small tin box he placed under his seat. I had a sinking feeling that my commission would never be paid. The greedy bastard. I kept telling myself that I should have given him only $360 and kept my $90. Live and learn, I thought.

Casually, I picked up the letter sent to him by the publisher in Alabama and memorized the address.

"What are you doing?" he asked suspiciously.

"Trying to see what they wrote about paying for commissions."

Jesús got upset. "Look, I helped you pass your Spanish class. I got this job for both of us, and it's my car we're using."

"Jesús, you're right. Add all those items up and tell me how much I owe you."

He didn't realize I was jesting.

"About ninety dollars," he said. "We're even and I won't need your help anymore. I gave you the better street and took the bad one."

"I won't object if you donate the money I earned to your parents' mission," I said, turning on my righteous face.

Preferring not to have a fight on his hands, he acted relieved and accepted my offer. "That's a good idea, I will send them the ninety dollars," he said reluctantly.

That same evening I wrote a letter to the Alabama publisher, saying that Jesús and I had sold eleven books: nine *Bibles* and two encyclopedias. I went on to offer my services as salesman to them for the region. I ended the letter by writing, "Please give my regards to the Lehmans when you write to the mission in Costa Rica. I rejoice in knowing that the ninety dollars of my commission (which I gave to their son Jesús, to donate to their mission) will be well used in the fields of the Lord. May God bless the Reverend and Mrs. Lehman." I kept a carbon copy of the letter.

Two weeks later I received a note from the Alabama publisher congratulating me on helping Jesús Lehman sell so many books in one day, adding that my letter was forwarded to the mission in Costa Rica. A month later another letter came from the publisher offering me a salesman's job.

Jesús had also received a letter from the publisher relieving him of his duties as a salesman for the company and asking him to hand over all remaining books to me. In all that time, he had sold only six *Bibles* and no encyclopedias. Furious at me while he handed over two crates full of books, he shouted, "You're a sneak and a double-crosser! You got me in trouble with my parents."

I showed him the copy of the letter I had sent the publisher. "You can see for yourself what a nice message I sent to your parents."

"I was slow to send the ninety dollars to them and they are very upset with me. I've prayed and the Lord will forgive me."

"Fine, I'm glad you spoke to Jesus, Jesús. And you can send the money now," I told him, "and be even with the Lord, whose ways are mysterious."

21

In the middle of my sophomore year, a miraculous event happened. I started a campaign, confiding first to Mr. Ernst, "I'm going to ask you to help me, Mr. Ernst. You must have special connections in Heaven."

He laughed. "Oh, I don't know about that, Dinky," he admitted somewhat shyly, "the good Lord has no favorites among His flock."

"I need a car badly to carry on with His work," I explained. "If you'd pray for me, God will answer for sure." I knew he'd spread my request among many people in the churches of the county.

I made my petition in front of a congregation of farmers in the town of Malone, not far from Heighman, where I had been called to deliver a $45 sermon. Answering someone's prayer convinces donors that they are in close proximity with God, which to most people is quite an honor, and perhaps the most remarkable accomplishment in their mediocre and insipid lives.

A week later I received a letter bearing a postmark and a return address from Malone. Written in what seemed to be a child's large and awkward handwriting, it read, "Dear Reverind Mister Dink: I was very ill last week when I heerd yu preach and promist if the Good Lord give me back my helth I would give yu one of my cars sinse yu need one and now I am good as new so I will keep my promis. Come and get it, in Christ." He scribbled his address and said in his P. S., "The '58 is runnin good."

When I showed the car to Mr. Ernst I said to him, "See what I meant about you having connections up in Heaven?" But, of course, I didn't believe in any miracles. For me, there's nothing mysterious, no heavenly rewards, no Hell. And after being around preachers of all sorts all my life, I am convinced that very few of them believe in that nonsense. If they did believe, they wouldn't be such cheats, such liars and fornicators, all of them tax evaders, breaking at least one of the commandments every day. And among priests of the other faith, child abusers.

Mr. Ernst ate all his meals at the college with the rest of us, students and single faculty and administrators. Four people sat at each table and one could sit wherever there was an empty chair. But few people would join Mr. Ernst until the last moment, when empty seats became unavailable. Mr. Ernst usually monopolized the conversation with a torrent of *Bible* quotes or some irrelevant set of observations. It took away one's appetite watching him shove big spoonfuls into his mouth. Coffee usually dribbled down his chin to his white shirt and food was dragged out of his open mouth by the cataract of words. Just to hear him slurp was nauseating enough not to want to sit by him.

Before sitting down, everyone stood in unison. A little bell rang for quiet and someone would say a few brief words of gratitude to the Lord for the meal we were about to consume.

One Monday morning, Mr. Ernst was in a state of great excitement. Face flushed, eyes bloodshot, hair in great disarray as though he had tossed in bed all night, Mr. Ernst took a spoon from the table and, instead of sitting down after the breakfast prayer with me and Chuck, repeatedly tapped it against an empty glass to call everyone's attention. "Brothers and sisters," he exclaimed, his body shaking, "I want to witness to the Holy Ghost's bounty. Last night He woke me, oh, the joy. The Holy Ghost took me by the hand to Paul and Silas, the first missionaries, who beckoned to me to join them in their mission to Macedonia, as it says in the sixteenth chapter of *The Acts*."

Mr. Ernst began to sob and then lost his balance. He grabbed for his chair but would have fallen to the floor if Chuck and I hadn't been quick enough to help him sit down. Before we knew it, he sprang up again and yelled, "The Holy Ghost commanded me: Come to Macedonia and help us!"

A few "Amens" were heard in the dining room, but most of the students shook their heads, some worried about Mr. Ernst's fragile condition; others, like myself and Chuck, doubting his sanity.

My many years of experience with Granny alerted me about how the Holy Ghost can wreak havoc among the faithful, nothing with which the faint of heart should fool around. Its mystical and nebulous nature could stir even the dullest imagination into unpredictable speculations and outrageous conclusions based strictly on personal projections. You had to be on high alert when dealing with the Holy Ghost. It's definitely not an undertaking for the indolent or the timid.

After his witnessing, I saw Mr. Ernst at the print shop and talked to him on company time. Knowing that there was a small town in the outskirts of Cleveland, Ohio, called Macedonia, I teased him, "So you're determined to become a missionary in Ohio, Mr. Ernst?"

"Ohio?" He was perplexed and stood there with his mouth open, still reeling from the emotional upheaval of his performance at the dining room. "I pastored a church in Ohio for two years before I studied printing, but never heard of a town named Macedonia in that state."

"Yes, there's one there and it's not too far from here," I noted. "A couple of hundred miles around the bend of Lake Erie. If you hurry you should be there by this evening, going through Mesopotamia."

"Mesopotamia?" he asked, slowly moving his head from side to side in disbelief. "That's somewhere in the Middle East, not Ohio," he said, recovering somewhat.

Geography being one of my areas of interest, I knew exactly what I was talking about. "Well, yes, Mr. Ernst, but there's a Mesopotamia in Ohio as well, right close to Macedonia, look at a map. Maybe that's where the Holy Ghost was leading you, a journey close to home."

Mr. Ernst started to laugh and a bit of drool escaped one corner of his mouth. "You are such a joker, Dinky. Macedonia, Ohio. Ha!"

"How do you know which Macedonia, which Mesopotamia Paul and Silas meant, Mr. Ernst?"

"Obviously they didn't mean Ohio," Mr. Ernst said. "Ohio wasn't even around for Paul and Silas to know about it. Dinky, you're pulling my leg."

"No, Mr. Ernst. I'm shocked that it comes right out of the blue, you going so far away. How are you going to get the money to go overseas?"

"The Lord will provide. Just like He provided your car." Mr. Ernst had a mischievous twinkle in his eye.

I was mystified because he seemed so cocky, possessed of a newly found self-assurance.

A couple of weeks later, Mr. Ernst approached me after chapel. "Dinky," he said, taking me by the arm and leading me where he could talk without being overheard. "I can tell that you are a young man who, in spite of limited experience, is quite clever about making his way in the world. I want to trust you with a special secret."

"Mr. Ernst, you can be sure I'll never reveal it. I give you my word."

With my fingers I gestured, putting a tight seal over my mouth.

"You asked me where I'd get the funds to go all the way to Macedonia," he said in a hushed voice, looking around to make sure nobody else was listening to his revelation. "Now, listen to me, Dinky, before I was born again, saved by God's grace, I was a champion pool player. I was also a champion of 18.1, 18.2 balk line and three-cushion billiards. I'll tell you about these sports some other time. I played with the best—with Maurice Vignaux of France, with Willie Hoppe, the child prodigy, in the Chicago world tournament of 1940. Before I was saved. I lost to both of them, but they were the world champs. The secret is that whenever there's an emergency and I need money for the Lord's work, I can go most anywhere and make a big bundle playing any variation of billiards. And I can give almost unbelievable odds to most players and still win. They see an odd, short, drooling old man with thick glasses and rumpled clothes and think I can't possibly beat them. But I still win whenever I want. And I can even make it look like my shots are flukes and I'm winning by sheer luck. My opponent would have to be world class to beat me and there aren't many of those around in the usual billiard parlors and taverns. I know the good Lord will forgive me. He knows I don't keep a cent for myself, but give it all to Him."

I was flabbergasted, my jaw hanging half a yard. It was hard for me to contain myself and I blurted out the first thing that popped in my head. "You, Mr. Ernst, the Lord's shark?"

"Yes," he said, the glint still shining in his eyes. "I've not told anyone and it's a weight off my shoulders to confide in you, Dinky. God bless you."

"While you're at it," I suggested, always ready to take advantage of the Lord's generosity, "get me a few bucks also, since I'm going to Colombia, South America, next summer, to work for the same Lord." A few weeks later Mr. Ernst gave me a couple of one hundred dollar bills and a wink. He called the gift a surplus from his pool earnings. I could tell he had made a killing in the pool halls because he was ready to buy the airline tickets.

While I was getting my things ready to go to the mission in Colombia, Mr. Ernst was making preparations for his call to Macedonia, a stronghold of the Greek Orthodox Church, a place difficult to penetrate by one solo missionary. But Mr. Ernst was undeterred by these superficial barriers, as he called them, and proceeded with his plans. After sending many letters to obscure congregations, he received a positive answer from the Holy Ghost's Light of the Cross Missionary Crusaders. They offered him room and board for three months in northern Greece, but no stipend for travel expenses. Mr. Ernst was overjoyed. He flashed his acceptance letter when I stepped into the print shop.

"I am now more certain than ever. Didn't I tell you? Look at this letter, Dinky," he said, shoving the letter in my face. "It's from a Holy Ghost church. Can you imagine that? It was the Holy Ghost who led me in the first place when He appeared to me with Paul and Silas. This letter is a confirmation. They're telling me that if I get the funds, I can join them in their mission this summer. I feel it in my bones—the Holy Ghost is in charge of this project."

When I saw the old black Studebaker he drove leave Heighman just before the weekend, I realized, with satisfaction, that I was the only one who knew that the old man sitting at the wheel was in search of any decadent pool hall where he might find some innocent hick who would lose what was in his jeans to the Lord's flimflammer.

22

By the end of spring, Chuck and I had over fifteen hundred dollars each from selling books. I never told him where I stashed my money. His was in a bank in Burlington, Vermont. Chuck's idea was to build a nest egg of at least three thousand dollars and then sail into some serious portfolio building.

"We could make money this summer selling *Bibles*," he said to me, "but I guess you're set on going to Colombia."

"I have to repay the Alliance, or else they'll end my scholarship. And I'll get college credit for working in the missions. As soon as I get back we'll continue in the book business."

On one of my trips to the bank in Montréal to deposit my earnings in my savings account, I discovered a jewelry store that was also a pawnshop, with a barred window in the corner for placing bets on horse races. I became acquainted with the owner, a friendly old man who loved to talk about horses and jewels. Mr. Lepinski expressed his interest in emeralds when I told him I was going to Colombia, South America.

"The stones from the Muzo mines in Colombia are famous all over the world for their clarity," he explained. He referred to gems as stones.

"You could teach me and then I'll get some good stones for you," I proposed, becoming rapidly interested.

"It's not as simple as you think. You must have experience also," he warned.

Mr. Lepinski brought out a couple of the gems mounted on rings that he had for sale and enumerated the signs of a good emerald. "But there's much more to learn." He paused, then pulled out a couple of pamphlets and a book from a drawer. "You can borrow these."

I was especially interested in the pictures of the gradations of shaded emeralds, which were faulty, to the most valuable, clear ones. I studied the photos upon my return to Heighman, and a month later, when I returned to Montréal, I wanted him to test my knowledge. I must have impressed him favorably because he asked me to bring him back a few stones.

"If they're good I might buy some, but I can't promise anything. You'll have to take your chances," Mr. Lepinski warned me.

Reverend Wesley sent me a bus ticket routed through Philadelphia instead of New York City, spoiling the vague idea I harbored to look up Mildred in the big city. I had an image of her standing by the neon sign of the dilapidated hotel, waiting to take me to the dark corridor under the staircase. But I really didn't mind.

I arrived at night at the bus station in Charleston, West Virginia, and saw Reverend Wesley's inimitable figure waiting for me at the Greyhound station when I got off the bus. Dark as it was, I couldn't make out who was standing next to him. It looked like a young woman dressed in a colorful and fashionable manner. I was puzzled, wondering who she might be, when all of a sudden she moved in a familiar way and I recognized the woman —it was the Reverend Sister Todd, my own Grandma! As I approached, she opened her arms and shouted, "My Dolly boy, haven't seen you in a coon's age. Here I am!"

I was astounded. She looked more like her daughter, my mother. She had lost so much weight, half of her was gone. Mentally, I started computing and realized that she must still be in her early fifties. Unbelievable, I thought, but the more I looked at them, the more obvious it became—the Reverend Doctor Wesley Neighbour and Sister Todd were now a couple. The thought of Old Cadaver humping my Granny didn't much appeal to me.

"What in Hades happened to you? Where did my plump Granny go?" I asked, somewhat angry at her for not being the comforting cushion she had always been.

"I feel much better, Doll. Since I lost that pork hog I used to lug around, I stopped taking the medications and I'm not feeling dizzy and loony anymore. The Reverend has helped me a lot." She sounded reasonable, but a little subdued. Had she traded her old fizz for sanity?

"Look, Doll," she said to me, flashing a ringed finger

in front of my face. "Now, I'm Mrs. Neighbour. We should of let you know, but we were in a mighty rush. We got married three days ago."

My God, I thought, Old Cadaver is my own Grandpa. I consoled myself knowing that I might gain a few advantages out of this union.

We took an early bus to Miami, the two honeymooners sitting close to each other during the whole trip. The next day we flew—Granny and I for the first time in our lives—on a DC4 over the Caribbean sea, stopping in Camagüey, Cuba, and then in Kingston, Jamaica, to let off and pick up passengers. With each landing, it was increasingly hot as we entered the tropical zone. Not long after leaving Jamaica, with a great body of land extending over the entire horizon, we were told the plane had crossed into the southern continent of the Americas. We flew over vast swamps, slowly emerging into a jungle with a river snaking through it. I was told that the name of the river was Magdalena. The landscape gradually changed into dryer land and finally into a highly elevated and corrugated mountain range, the Andes. I kept looking below, enthralled by the spectacle of lush fields. We landed in the epicenter of this greenery, in Medellín, the main industrial city of Colombia, and capital of the province, located in a beautiful valley completely surrounded by high mountains.

One of the local pastors, Reverendo Don Julio Bolívar, a short, pale man with a thick mustache that contrasted with his balding head, came to take us to a mission in Ratonpelao, a town at the top of one of the highest mountain peaks surrounding the city. He spoke in a high-pitched voice with a commanding tone that took everyone by surprise. When he realized that Granny and I didn't understand a word he said in Spanish, he spoke in English, every word clearly enunciated so that what came out was most comprehensible in spite of his heavy accent. Once he saw that Granny and I were appendages of Reverend Wesley, he addressed most of his comments to him.

As we approached the outskirts of the village, Don Julio said, "There's something strange going on in Ratonpelao. Everybody stops and stares at us." He indicated a lady on the street, looking at us before she quickly pulled her child toward her, as though she wanted to protect him from us. "I don't like this. Something's not right here in Ratonpelao," he exclaimed. Julio liked to repeat the name of the village, which in English means "a peeled mouse."

Although the distance from the airport to the village, through the winding and narrow roads, was not over forty miles, it took us three hours to get there.

Upon arriving at the compound, we saw four missionary wives in an uproar, pleading on their knees, while several small children, blonde and blue-eyed, ran wildly about, the youngest ones naked. When they saw us get out of the station wagon, they stopped their invocation and approached us, great worry reflected in their eyes. The oldest woman, who seemed to be the leader of the group, introduced herself as Mrs. Douglas, from College Park, Georgia. "Our husbands are in the fields!"

Her husband was away for several days, converting people along the Magdalena River, the region we had just flown over, with some of the poorest and most abandoned communities in the country.

She explained to us that a mob of peasants had shot bullets at the mission house till dawn after the Catholic priest had promised at a Mass eternal salvation to those who'd reject the intrusion of the Protestant missionaries. No one was hurt, but they terrorized the women and children, broke every window, and cut all electric and telephone wires. A barn that was close to the house had been burned to the ground.

"That happened last Sunday, three nights ago," Mrs. Douglas said with an unmistakable southern drawl. "We wish you had arrived before the attack. Thank the Lord you're here."

"Did you find out what else the priest said to them?" Reverend Wesley inquired.

"He said that those who would get rid of the Protestant heathens, as they call us, would receive their reward in Heaven, sit next to God's throne through eternity."

It surprised me when Reverend Bolívar came over and said, "Shooting at us, eh? I know how to deal with these kinds of attacks. We must defend ourselves. We're all hot-blooded. I need to go back to Medellín and bring reinforcements so this will not happen again."

Don Julio left the compound in a hurry, before dark.

I was intrigued by an enormous cage jammed with parrots, parakeets, and other exotic tropical birds. There hardly seemed to be room for one more. I learned from one of the missionary ladies that Mrs. Douglas had a side business—shipping birds to Georgia. Every time I walked by the cage I felt ill at ease. The idea of me being caged in a prison was going through my mind. It was the one thing I wanted to avoid.

Later, I asked Mrs. Douglas about her project. She giggled and said, "A missionary friend of mine has an airplane and travels back and forth to Atlanta twice a month and takes one of the cages with birds on each trip. I provide good homes in the States for the poor creatures. It's good for pocket money too, and we give the tithe to our church." Mrs. Douglas excused herself. "I must attend now to Dolores's sores. She's our maid, rescued from prostitution in the streets of Medellín's slums."

She proceeded to call out for Dolores. A tall, black woman, about twenty-five years old, appeared. Mrs. Douglas embraced her rather possessively, to the woman's discomfort, and led her to a chair in front of a big bucket full of soapy, steaming water. The missionary knelt beside Dolores and proceeded to wash the sores on her feet. Mrs. Douglas began reciting a Biblical verse in Spanish and urged Dolores to repeat it.

"I've been trying to teach her the 23rd Psalm, but I

don't think her spirit is in it yet," Mrs. Douglas told us. "Often these blacks have a hard head. Nothing new gets through there." Mrs. Douglas snickered, pointing at her own head. Dolores, realizing she was talking about her, pouted and looked the other way, though she kept her feet in the warm water and allowed Mrs. Douglas to continue her soothing treatment.

While Mrs. Douglas continued with her chore as good Samaritan, she yelled out, "Bobby! Bobby! Bobby!"

A somewhat taciturn, gangly adolescent came out of one of the rooms that led to the patio where we were gathered. "Yes, Mother?" the boy said, yawning. "What you want now?"

"Dear, will you bring me that white bottle from the bathroom? It has a medication for Dolores's feet. And don't forget to prepare your lesson on *Lamentations* for your father. He'll be back in a couple of days and will want to hear your recitation, and you know how exacting he is." Bobby frowned, shrugged his shoulders and went on his errand.

Don Julio returned at dawn, driving the mission's bus. When he came close he explained, "Four missionaries are hidden under a canvas in the bus so no one could see them when we entered the village. Quite likely the villagers will attack again if they think there are only women and children here."

The four missionaries—all big men—slithered out of the vehicle, each one carrying a rifle and several rounds of ammunition. Two of them came into the mission house, one positioned himself in the bushes behind the house, and the fourth went to a tool shed a few yards from the burned barn. Don Julio made several trips to the bus, returning to distribute ammunition and pistols to the four men. Reverend Wesley refused a pistol. "No, I am a man of peace, Don Julio," he said, "and neither I, my wife, nor Richard here will bear arms. But we'll pray for you."

Luckily, though the men stayed for the rest of the week—praying, with guns in hand—the assailants didn't show up. The American missionaries who had come in the bus returned to Medellín the following Monday.

Reverend Wesley was saddened by the whole affair. Expressing his views didn't help his popularity among the other preachers. "To kill or wound an enemy is not what the Gospel tells us to do," he scolded them. Don Julio especially was upset and kept repeating that only he was in a position to know the best way to deal with his countrymen.

"Harming even one of them would not only jeopardize the whole missionary effort in South America," Reverend Wesley went on, "but endanger the souls of the missionaries. We must set an example, especially in a host country, where there's so much violence."

I overheard one missionary whisper, "I wish Wesley would stick to his violin playing instead of meddling in our problems. Julio knows best how to deal with his people."

I asked Granny how she felt about missionaries taking up arms to defend their compound. "The Reverend and I see eye-to-eye on the issue. Besides, you shoot one of them and the rest will slaughter you," she said to me. "And, by the way, aren't you glad all the birds are gone?"

The previous night, while everyone waited for the assault, someone had opened Mrs. Douglas's birdcage and it was completely empty in the morning. I looked at Granny. "You didn't, huh?"

"Don't tell on me, Dolly!" She slapped her thigh, laughed uproariously and placed her index finger over her lips. "Not even the Reverend knows, but I had to do it."

Before Don Julio took the four missionaries and most of the guns and rifles back to Medellín, he looked around suspiciously and said, "I think Dolores informed them about our presence here. A whore like that from the Medellín slums could easily betray us."

After the Reverend Bolívar left, Dolores was the only one at the mission who spoke Spanish fluently. Since one of the objectives of my stay in that country was to learn the language, Reverend Wesley asked her if she'd help me out, saying that she would know the popular, everyday language of the streets.

Reverend Douglas was scheduled to stay a few days in Ratonpelao and then take Reverend Wesley, Granny, and me to the river mission. I was supposed to learn a few expressions in Spanish, enough to get around, and

Dolores was put in charge of the intensive, total immersion three-day crash course.

Tienes muchos dólares? was one of her first questions to me when we were alone. She gave me a long, oblique and dark look. I understood mucho dollars for sure, and by the way she looked at me I figured out what she was after. I put out my right hand, waving my five fingers. She smiled knowingly and nodded. That evening, after the Spanish lessons and dinner, while everyone was asleep, Dolores quietly entered my room and got her first five bucks after she displayed her Latin American version of frenching.

Just before her husband's arrival, Mrs. Douglas had the worst experience of her life. Desperately searching for her diamond engagement ring that had disappeared from her dresser, she finally found it under a pile of clothes in Dolores's room. When Mrs. Douglas confronted her, Dolores stood in front of the frail missionary and slapped her in the face, knocking her down.

"How could she hit me?" Mrs. Douglas kept asking disconsolately. "Dolores looked at me with the most hatred I have ever seen in anyone's eyes," she said, awash in tears.

When Reverend Douglas arrived, he asked Dolores why she had hit someone who cared so much for her.

"If I cared for anyone, I wouldn't mind if they borrow one of my rings, but Mrs. Douglas called me a thief and that I'm not, even though I am a *puta*," Dolores said. Such was the translation that was made to those of us who didn't speak Spanish.

Dolores not only continued my Spanish lessons in the late afternoons, but also came in the dark of night to my room, as though nothing had happened. But on the third night I turned her down, displeased with my need of her. When I said, *"No gracias,"* she shrugged her shoulders and, to my relief, never came back. I was confident she wouldn't rat on me. And if she had, who would believe a *puta* from the slums?

23

An unexpected but very different type of violence beseeched the Douglas family during our trip to Puerto Berrío. From Medellín, we took the 6 a.m. train and arrived at the river port at 4 p.m. It was a slow, 115-mile train ride.

Throughout the trip to Puerto Berrío, Reverend Douglas, a strong man with an overwhelming physique, asked his son, Bobby, questions about the book of *Lamentations*, many of which Bobby couldn't answer. This displeased the father, who explained the meaning of obtuse passages, while the boy looked away to the more interesting landscape. On several occasions he was scolded for not paying attention.

"Dad, please, I want to enjoy this trip, not be pestered all the time. It's so annoying."

"You be careful how you talk to your father, young man."

A sullen silence followed, and father and son didn't speak to each other again for hours while the train made its way across the Andean mountains. Granny whispered to me, "The boy should tell him to go suck eggs. That jerk ain't got sense enough to carry guts to a bear."

I noticed that when Bobby felt safe from his parents' prying eyes, he moved to the third class cars, to smoke a cigarette, an act of defiance that would have gained him a horrible scolding from his father had he seen it.

The following day, we were all sitting in the chapel that also was used as living room at the new mission, and Reverend Douglas demanded again a response from Bobby. "This is the last time I'm going to ask you, boy. How do you explain, within the context of the whole book of *Lamentations of Jeremiah*, the 20th verse of its first chapter, where it says, 'My heart is turned within me; for I have grievously rebelled'? Hmmmm?"

When the boy looked away in defiance, Reverend Douglas grabbed his shoulders, shook him and said, "Jeremiah felt guilty for rebelling against God and eliciting punishment well deserved. That's what it means to any dumbbell." Granny turned to me at that moment and whispered, "Thare he blows!"

Bobby pried loose from his father's grasp, fury distorting his youthful face, and leaped upon the open *Bible*, screaming, "I don't give a damn about your *Lamentations*!"

The father, startled at the boy's outburst, was unable to stop him from ripping the *Bible*'s pages. Mrs. Douglas screamed to heaven while the father tried to keep calm, invoking the old, overused admonition that so many preachers like to hurl when they are in a tight spot, to feel superior. "Forgive him, Lord, for he knows not what he's doing."

Bobby got even more furious. "Sanctimonious crap! I do know what I'm doing!" And finally, pulling off the hard cover that had resisted his first destructive effort, he threw it against his father's chest, sobbing, "I know what I'm doing. I'm ripping up your damn *Bible* and don't want to have any more to do with it, or you!"

Bobby's mother went over to him, attempting to place her consoling arms around him, but he made a brusque movement, rejecting her, and went to sit on an empty bench. "You should of left me in the States with all my friends," he mumbled. He looked up accusingly at his parents, unable to stop crying, and vented his anger among sobs that burst out sporadically in a most anguished manner. "You shouldn't of ... brought me ... to this malaria-infested ... place ... and force me .... I am sick and tired of ... hearing *Bible* talk ... night and day."

Hard as they tried to put Humpty Dumpty together again, it didn't work. Bobby stopped talking to his parents, hoping to wear them out so they'd send him back to Georgia, which did occur a few weeks later.

The following day was a religious holiday and those who had shown interest in joining the new mission in Puerto Berrío came to the service led by Reverend Douglas. His wife played the piano and sang a few solos. Reverend Wesley played his violin. I was introduced as a student of Theology who might be interested in becoming a full-fledged missionary in Colombia. Bobby went to the river to watch some fishermen, and the loading and unloading of the colorful paddle-wheel ships.

Nine natives, most of them dockworkers and their families, attended the services. Mrs. Douglas served a picnic lunch while her husband filmed the event. He wanted everyone filing into the chapel to run out the back door, put on a different poncho or hat or coat, and return to the front, to enter the chapel again. The participants took this suggestion as an entertaining new game and went around re-entering the chapel on three or four occasions, each time changing their appearance. Some wore dark glasses on their second entry, or took off their shoes and entered barefoot the third time around. On film, it looked like there had been more than sixty people entering. Reverend Douglas confided that the folks back home would feel enthusiastic watching a large congregation and would be more inspired by such a successful mission. Of course, I knew that he was just trying to get larger donations from watchers back home.

We stayed in Puerto Berrío four days before returning to Medellín. The Alliance had progressed during the last two years more than any other group of missionaries in Latin America. Its new headquarters overseas was located next to a small stream, on land extending up the mountainside toward its peak. The limits of the vast property were marked on all sides by eucalyptus trees whose delicate fragrance permeated the grounds. Coffee beans and orchids were harvested by a few recently saved peasants.

On one of the many hills on the property was a corral with black and white cattle, thoroughbred imports from Ecuador, providing the missionaries with excellent, high quality meat. A few goats were loose to mow the grounds next to the main office building, where Reverend Wesley spent most of his time. No lawn mower could have done a better job than was done by those goats.

Granny and I were taking a walk one afternoon and came upon a boy who displayed his bullfighting technique with one of the larger billy goats, using a red shirt for a cape. The goat repeatedly ran into the red shirt while the boy got as close to the charging animal as he dared. It looked so simple that Granny wanted to try, but the boy was leery. "*Puede ser peligroso,*" he warned her.

"Granny," I said, "he's saying that it could be dangerous." But Granny disregarded the warning and grabbed the shirt out of the boy's hands. I kept out of the way.

During the first furious onslaught the goat made at her, his stubby and powerful horns grazed her stomach so closely that the boy applauded and yelled, "*Olé, olé, olé!*" I joined him in cheering after the equally close second pass. But at the third one, Granny's attention wavered as she saw Reverend Wesley come out of the building and head toward us. The goat butted her with a full blast in her groin and sent her rolling on the ground. The boy ran after the red shirt to try to engage the goat's attention in a different direction, but was too late. As Granny was getting up with difficulty, holding on to her side in obvious pain, the goat thundered passed the boy and crashed his hard head against her butt, throwing her into the bushes. Reverend Wesley and I came to Granny's rescue and pulled her out of the brambles, from where she appeared all scratched up with a few sprouts of blood.

"That puts a definite end to my billy goat fighting career," she told us, gingerly touching with the palms of her hands the sore places and drying the drops of blood running down her arms.

The boy's father came to apologize. "I ask many pardon for mine boy," he told Granny. "It is not good give you shirt to fight bad animal. I am very sorry."

"I was the foolish one. Not your son," Granny told him. And I heard Reverend Wesley say under his breath, "Amen to that."

Granny had a lapel button in her pocket with the image of Donald Duck and gave it to the man. "Souvenir for the boy," she said to him.

The man took the tin button, put it on the palm of his hand and closely examined it. "Oh, sank you, sank you very, very moch."

While Granny limped away—by Reverend Wesley's side—to their quarters, the boy's father invited me to come see his *Unites Estate* collection.

We walked up the hill to a two-room house, painted white, with a banana leaf roof, surrounded by a couple of other huts, all made out of cow dung. Four small children, all of them naked, played outside the house while his wife washed the missionaries' clothes a few paces from where a small stream gurgled. "I will be Pastor after study one year. Maybe preach in Unites Estate," he said to me.

His son, wearing the red shirt, approached us and whispered something to his father. "No, not now, I busy with Reverend," the man said to the boy, pointing at me while he spoke. "Mister Reverend, my name Rodrigo Restrepo," he said, shaking my hand effusively. "Come now, I show you mine collection."

We walked into the house, dark and miserably furnished, with several mattresses strewn on the earthen floor. At eye level, a wood shelf was attached to the farthest wall. On top of it, and as the centerpiece, stood a large empty bottle of Coca-Cola. It was surrounded by a small Confederate flag made of paper sticking out of a bottle of empty Alka Seltzer with a small yellow and green banner with Heighman College printed on it; a picture of an emaciated Jesus bleeding on the cross; a Sears & Roebuck yo-yo; a folded napkin with the Waldorf Astoria logo; a miniature *Bible* in English; a postcard with the picture of the Empire State Building with a copper replica of the Statue of Liberty leaning on it; and a tiny portrait of Dwight Eisenhower in uniform. Above this collection, pinned against the wall, were a small U.S. flag and a used train ticket from Miami to Atlanta.

I was surprised when the man approached me with a mischievous grin and asked, "You know if true or not true Coca-Cola factory put coca powder in bottles?" I shrugged my shoulders and answered with my scant knowledge of Spanish, "*Quien sabe,* señor. *Es posible.*" We both laughed.

The man hesitated, not knowing exactly where to put the Donald Duck button. "Where you sink, Reverend, I put my Donald Duck? Here or here?" he asked, moving the pin from one end of the board to the other.

Squinting, I looked at the board as though it were a work of art. "Let me see," I said, pretending to be in grave conflict. "It would look best, in my opinion, right here on top of your Coca-Cola bottle, Reverend Restrepo." The man practically swooned when he heard the appellative. He took a deep breath and placed—with trembling hand—his new icon where I had suggested.

Unfortunately, it slid through the opening of the bottle and disappeared. It rattled against the glass as he first turned the bottle upside down and then tried to shake it out. But the small Donald Duck button got stuck on its way out somewhere near the neck of the bottle. After fussing with the thing for a few minutes, he gave up. "Sank you very moch. I try more tomorrow," he said, forcing a smile. And then he made his promise: "With God help I will make Donald Duck come out. If go in, it come out again."

Watching him, it occurred to me that shortly after missionaries distributed their Bibles throughout the Latin American continent, Coca-Cola and other U.S. products had made their appearance. They worked in tandem to stupefy the ignoramus populace. "Drink Coke and be saved!" I now understood why these companies were so fond of supporting obscure Protestant cults´ missions.

The result was right in front of me in the form of Reverend-to-be Don Rodrigo Restrepo's awe for all things from the U.S.A., a condition that was slowly spreading throughout the born-again green continent. Never mind who was in charge in our nation, Democrats or Republicans; the real battle for the wealth of these less developed nations was taking place in the cultural and religious change we missionaries and industrialists were implanting. That's where the money was to be had.

I was assigned to work at WACO's print shop, located in downtown Medellín. After working two years as apprentice to Mr. Ernst, I knew how to do most of the work a printer did, plus bookbinding, although my skill with linotypes was still raw.

When the Alliance wanted to expand its educational services in Colombia, the best vehicle was using small publications such as newsletters, leaflets and pamphlets. It was too costly to have the material printed by others, so the Alliance planned to import the machinery from the States and set up its own press. An appropriate, inexpensive place was selected—an abandoned building next to a market in a deteriorating district near the railroad station. To get to the print shop I had to walk through streets full of taverns with blaring music from jukeboxes and with such unique names as Venus's Mound, Sinners' Paradise, The Pharaoh's Den and People's Harem. It was easy to pick any of the women loitering about and spend a few minutes in a dilapidated room in the back of a tavern for a couple of pesos. I never had to go back to the same prostitute twice.

Exploring the area, I found a small park tucked between buildings where men sold contraband emeralds and other black market merchandise. The illegal business was carried on night and day. After a few visits, I invested four hundred dollars from my savings on a lot of five emeralds from Muzo, which, to the seller, seemed like a fortune in Colombian pesos. To sweeten the deal, he threw in a handful of what he called "trash," very small, unpolished, dark green rocks that, he said, could be mounted on cheap rings, bracelets or earrings.

The printing press arrived from Charleston soon after we came to the city and was set up in the rented building, but when the missionaries went to the Department of Business and Industry to register the print shop, they ran into trouble. The law required that the owner be a Colombian citizen. The Reverend Don Julio Bolívar was selected. He had worked for the Alliance during the last five years and lived in a house next to the church with his family of seven children and his pregnant wife.

During his formative years Don Julio had studied at a Jesuit seminary and stayed in that order for several years. His conversion to Protestantism was the object of severe criticism in his native city, where he couldn't stay for fear of continued punishment by the ecclesiastic authorities.

On paper, Don Julio was the owner of the print shop even though he had separate contracts with the mission in which he appeared only as an employee and not as an owner. His duty at the printing office was a sham. He came to the shop once a week to sign papers and was paid a small sum of money in addition to his regular salary as Pastor. In Colombia that sort of employment was called "a necktie job"—the hired person did nothing.

My job for the rest of the summer was to teach a group of recently saved Colombians how to accomplish the tasks needed for the operation of the print shop. The management was left in the hands of Andrew Michaels, a Heighman College graduate who had majored in Business Administration and Spanish. Michaels was what they referred to as a "business missionary" and had no pastoral duties. He was a tall Yankee from Maine with a disdainful attitude toward those he called "the natives." He was so fluent in Spanish that all the missionaries, including me, frequently consulted him about the language. All the letters and documents the print shop sent out were written by him. When the manager found Don Julio reading one of the documents he was supposed to sign, he confronted him. "Reverend Bolívar, there's no need for you to read these papers we have you sign. They are the Alliance's business."

"I don't sign anything unless I read it," was Don Julio's curt answer.

After a couple of weeks I got to know Don Julio better. He had studied with the Jesuits and was educated well enough to debate obscure theological issues. It was rumored among the missionaries that Don Julio had the best Biblical knowledge of any Colombian they had met. Even Reverend Wesley consulted him on difficult theological questions that were in contention between Catholics and Protestants. Since I was usually available to him in the print shop, he found it convenient to practice English with me.

One morning Don Julio came into the shop very distraught. He had been crying.

"What's happened, Don Julio?" I asked in English.

He shook his head and was silent for a long time. Then he took out a handkerchief to blow his nose and dry tears he could not hold back. "My little daughter," he said, choosing to speak to me in Spanish. "She drown in a swamp. She now with the Lord, but we are very, very sad."

"So sorry." I didn't know what else to say to the man.

"I am glad you tell me you sorry for my family," he said, choking and unable to look at me. "I very grateful many pray for me now, but...." He stopped and didn't finish what he had in mind.

The next time we saw each other he said, "I have mental retarded boy, and doctors' expenses, special education, *medicinas* so *caro*, I don't know how I can live."

I asked him if he couldn't ask for a raise and he told me that, since he was the highest paid Colombian pastor in the Alliance, it would be most unlikely for them to increase his salary. I was curious and, putting good manners aside, asked him how much he received.

"Six hundred Colombian pesos a month, and I can use a small house, very near to swamps."

During his next visit to the print shop, as he was reading a document he was to sign, Don Julio came across the salary made by Andrew Michaels: $900 per month, plus housing, maid service, medical expenses, one month of vacation each year with roundtrip travel to the States, retirement benefits, and a generous allowance for food. Other documents showed the salaries made by the missionaries living in Medellín and those up in Ratonpelao. They ranged between $600 for the least experienced ones who had just finished their training, up to $2,000 per month for the veterans, all receiving the same perks as Michaels, all of them having access to cars. And they were all paid in U.S. dollars, not Colombian pesos.

Don Julio was very angry when he came over to me later and said, "If they don't pay me more I have to do something they don't like. My family need food."

During my last day of the interesting summer I spent in Colombia, I learned that Don Julio had been given a raise of 100 pesos a month—a miserly raise of thirty-three U.S. dollars—and a better house, away from the swamp. Don Julio continued posing as the owner of the print shop to fulfill the requirements of the law. But in the middle of the second semester of my junior year at Heighman College, I got a letter from him saying that he wanted to set the record straight by telling me he had claimed possession of the print shop as the rightful owner and abandoned his pastoral duties with the Alliance because he had to make a living for his family, rather than continue being exploited as slave labor. The Alliance lost a print shop and I learned a valuable lesson: Exploitation of those who are under you has to be done sensibly so they won't rebel.

24

I drove to Montréal and paid a visit to Lepinski's Jewelry and Pawn Shop. Mr. Lepinski was glad to see me.

"Well, did you bring me any emeralds from Colombia?" he wanted to know.

I took off my money belt and smiled at him. "I will show you first the good ones," I said, undoing the threads that held the belt together.

I had declared nothing at Customs when entering the States and Canada. Nobody suspected anything. Why would they suspect a ministerial student? After all, I was lily white, tall, blonde and athletic, a good-looking blue-eyed young fellow, with well-placed dimples on my cheeks, and a smiling face that seemed to be without a worry in the world. Why would they suspect me of trying to smuggle emeralds into the country? They let me through without comment.

"Here are the five gems, Mr. Lepinski," I said, placing each one on the black velvet where they displayed their verdant glow, looking more beautiful than before. The expert put them under his magnifying glass. He mumbled something to himself that I didn't understand, shined a harsh light on each of them, tilted his head to look from a different angle, and placed them in two groups of two each, with the fifth gem in between.

"Just like a dice showing five dots," I said, knowing his predilection for betting. Mr. Lepinski disregarded my comment. I spread out the twenty unpolished stones on the table and saw him wince as he looked at them.

"Out of the five you're showing off only two are in good shape," he said, still wearing over his nose the magnifying glass that showed his eye enlarged. "But I bet they cheated you with the other three. I hope you didn't pay much for the lot. The two top ones are in fairly good condition. And the one in the middle is OK. The twenty unpolished ones, what they call *basura* in Colombia, are also garbage here in Canada. How much did you invest in this deal?"

I lied without batting an eye. "This lot of five, plus what you and the Colombians call garbage, cost me eight hundred U.S. dollars. Did they rob me?" I said, exactly doubling the amount I had paid.

The man started laughing. Finally, he blurted out, "The fools who sold you this lot don't have the foggiest notion about the gem business. They're worse off than you are. The poorest two gems you've shown me should be with the pile of garbage, the whole bunch hardly worth the mounting. The one in the middle might be worth fifty dollars. But the top two are easily worth eight hundred each, what you said you paid for the lot. For the whole bunch, I will give you the equivalent of $1,200 U.S., Rich. And I'm being generous."

After I deposited the money in the bank, I looked for a shoe manufacturer that would make me two pairs of very elegant shoes that would add a couple of inches to my height. Since the school year was just starting, fellow students and faculty would attribute my spurt of growth to the good Colombian food the missionaries had fed me. I was convinced that the taller a man, the greater attention and respect he receives. And that's Power.

Bad news came from the mission in Colombia. Civil unrest and widespread revolt throughout the countryside were daily occurrences. I didn't understand the reason for so much violence in Colombia until I met the *marrano*, the pig.

Five months after my return from South America, in the middle of my junior year, I met a new transfer student. Mr. Ernst—still buoyed by having converted three Macedonians the previous summer, even though two of them had backslid before his return—always interested in being the first to meet students who came through foreign missions, introduced us.

"This is Dinky," he said, "and this is Pepe. Pepe just came from Colombia and, since both of you spent last summer there, you might have lots to talk about."

José Vieira Cano told me he was a Catholic and a medical student. Later, when we got to know each other better, he told me how he had arrived at H. C. "My father sent me to a medical school in Caracas. After I passed the first years' courses with flying colors, I was celebrating in my room, when my father—an old-fashioned Jew with deep convictions—came unannounced to visit me and found me in the arms of a *jamona*. He immediately took me back to Colombia."

"What's a *jamona*?" I asked.

"A good looking, older woman, with large breasts." He winked at me.

The father told the young man that in a good religious college in the United States his foolish passions might be tamed. At the American Embassy, the old man was informed about the whereabouts of missionaries stationed in Colombia and the name of Heighman College appeared with some frequency in their recommendations.

Pepe found himself transplanted from a prominent medical school in one of the most cosmopolitan cities in Latin America to the solitude of the Adirondacks and the austerity of H. C. within a few days. With his record of science courses being as good as it was he was granted full credit for his year at the school in Caracas. The fact that he was fluent in English made it easier for him to be accepted. Without too much effort, Pepe got mostly A's at H. C. and everyone thought he was a genius.

A few months after Pepe arrived, another revival meeting took place in Heighman. Pepe attended and had a very visible salvation experience. Certainly it wasn't quite as dramatic as the one put on by Bob López, but without the speaking in tongues and inordinate yelling and writhing on the ground, it was still a climactic event for the local people to see their newest foreign student's rebirth.

The following Saturday, after the revival meeting, Chuck and I found Pepe hitchhiking in Vermont. We were no longer going to the movies in Plattsburgh and went to Burlington instead, a much bigger town where there were taverns and dance halls galore and no one from Heighman would see us.

Shortly after he got in the car, Pepe flashed a pack of Chesterfield cigarettes he pulled out of his pocket and, to our surprise, said, "I trust my intuition, and my intuition tells me to trust you. You care for one?"

After seeing a movie together, Pepe cheerfully joined Chuck and I for a glass of beer at a tavern and accepted our invitation to go square dancing. He insisted on paying for everything: cigarettes, the movie, beer, and tickets to the dance. "I'm on a very generous scholarship supplied by the coffee growers of my hometown in Colombia," he explained.

I nudged him in the ribs with my pointed elbow. *"Hombre, qué te pasó?"* I blurted out, my Spanish considerably improved, no longer needing Jesús Lehman's assistance. Pepe immediately knew what I was miffed about.

"I gave them what they wanted," he said.

"Be careful," Chuck advised him. "They spy on you."

"I went all the way," Pepe told us. "Now I have both my Catholic and Protestant credentials, for either the south or the north. The Protestants accept you if you bear witness by testifying in public, the Catholics if you let them baptize you and bow to their priest. Both are very impressed by such farce." He laughed and shook his head as though he couldn't believe the stupidity of the two religions.

Three months later, Pepe revealed his secret to me. "You know, Ricardo," he told me while we jogged near the campus one day, "I am a *Marrano*." I didn't understand and waited for an explanation, knowing that *marrano* meant the disdained pig in Spanish.

He stopped jogging and led me from the path we were following in the forest to a large boulder by the entrance to the campus, where we sat.

"Not even in Pereira, my hometown in Colombia, do people know that both sides of my family come from *Marranos*."

"Pepe, *marranos* is the word for pigs, isn't it?"

"Yes, it is!" he said emphatically, squinting his eyes while he looked at me straight. "I've never told anyone. My father would kill me if he knew I told you."

"During the Spanish Inquisition," he began, "the millions of Spanish and Portuguese Sephardic Jews were given a choice between death by burning or conversion to Catholicism. Those who converted under such stressful circumstances and their descendants, the *conversos*, were carefully watched for generations by the ecclesiastic authorities of Rome to find out if they had really meant their conversion or had only tried to save their lives by publicly trading their Jewish religion for Catholicism. That's why the most extreme and fanatical anti-Semitic Catholics were found among the *conversos*. They wanted to demonstrate to all how faithful they were and save their skins, even denying their background to their children to avoid being persecuted. But the *conversos* who continued practicing Judaism in secret were called pigs, the *Marranos*, a name we finally adopted with great pride after many decades of suffering. For centuries, the Office of the Inquisition in America, which was headquartered in Cartagena, Colombia, oversaw the execution of *Marranos* and anyone who didn't consent to the absolute power of the Holy Faith."

Pepe stopped talking to catch his breath. It seemed as if he could not stop talking as he revealed for me a secret that had been kept in his family for so many years.

"I'm convinced that this barbarous Inquisition, so widely imposed as the law in Colombia for such a long time, left a legacy of violence in the people, perverting the country's inhabitants because it was carried out by the priests, who represented the conscience. These priests in charge of the Inquisition in the New World made the use of violence the main means of effecting political change in Colombia. Ever since that time, my country has suffered violence more than any other in the continent.

They're at it again, killing one another in Colombia. Both sides of my family passed as Catholics for centuries—the Vieiras on my father's side from Portugal, and the Canos on my mother's side from Spain—but we secretly kept the Jewish traditions alive at home. I am a *Marrano*, a Jew who has to behave in Colombia like a Catholic, and now, to suit these Protestants, pass for one here since I was so ostensibly saved." Pepe laughed sardonically.

Pepe was opening my eyes to something that people in Colombia didn't dare speak about for fear of excommunication from the Church. He told me religious services were held weekly by his parents in their home for the few families of *Marranos* remaining.

"The Jews of the city, and even recent Jewish immigrants from Europe," he said, "ostracized us also, suspecting we had abandoned their religion and betrayed them. In this business of religion you can get hated from all sides."

I was self-satisfied that he should have such trust in someone he had only recently met. I had a natural ability to garner people's confidence and good will. It was something Granny had encouraged during my childhood by often saying, "You are so good looking and your eyes look so pure and innocent, my child, that you can get people to do whatever you want by just smiling at them. And don't forget to look them straight in the eyes."

Pepe couldn't stand the rigors of Heighman College. When the school year ended he left the village, never to return. A few months later I received a picture postcard from San Francisco, saying he had found work washing test tubes at a laboratory.

For many years I didn't know Pepe's whereabouts, until one day in the 1980s when I was already well into my work as an evangelizing radio and TV revivalist. I came across a publication detailing the new religious congregations that had been established in the country during the past year. There I saw in bold letters, "Rabbi Josech Cano, Sharee Torah Synagogue, a Messianic Jewish Temple, San Diego, California. A *Marrano* congregation returning to its early faith. Services in English and Spanish."

I phoned the synagogue. Pepe answered my call. He was delighted to hear from me. We had a long talk.

He had dropped his father's family name and kept his mother's. In spite of his efforts as a leader in his religious movement, the struggle to gain acceptance as a Jew by the conventional branches of Judaism was not forthcoming. He was recognized as a Jew only among a small group of Messianic Jews. They followed all the Judaic principles of Pepe's Sephardic ancestors with an additional detail—"We believe," Pepe conveyed to me, "that the Messiah, whose return to save the world we still await with you, is the gentle Jew from Nazareth, Rabbi Yeshua Ho Masehiach, who had taught only love, known later throughout the world as the revered Jesus Christ of Naz-areth, in whose name my forefathers were maligned, tortured and exterminated."

His exposition was enough to convince me that if I'd give him some support it would not elicit the ire of my organization. His was over three hundred families already, and with the enthusiasm he exuded there was no telling how far he'd go.

Pepe spoke as though he were in financial distress. I had one of my secretaries help him out with a gift of twenty thousand dollars. Pepe was most grateful and told me he'd use the money to buy a new car he badly needed to carry on his work.

Long ago I had reached the conclusion that a curious miracle occurs when you put in your pocket any religious leader: the rest of the group—the flock, following the shepherd—will fall in line. And I needed many sheep to fall in line in order to carry out my secret plans to gain ultimate Power.

25

The Weekly Student's office was a small room across the hall from the print shop on the ground floor of the main building on the Heighman College campus. Each student-reporter had a key to the office but had been warned by the editor to use the room just for newspaper business. On Wednesdays and Thursdays the room was full of aspiring journalists finishing their articles before the deadline for the Friday publication. Weekends to Wednesday it was as empty as a church on a Monday morning.

I wrote my column on Sundays. Every Monday morning, before eight o'clock classes, I'd open the paper's office and drop my little masterpiece in the editor's incoming mailbox. On one of those occasions, earlier than usual, Chuck accompanied me.

We were about to leave the room when we heard a tap. When the tapping got louder we went to the window and discovered one of the new co-eds. She was avoiding being seen by people walking near the building, hiding behind the bushes below the window. Seeing us, she lifted one arm, indicating she wanted to be let in. We opened the window and helped her climb to the sill.

"Hi, fellows," she greeted us as she slid into the room, laughing, mischief written all over her attractive face, unconcerned about her skirt coming up clear to her waist, while Chuck and I gawked at her shapely thighs. As we were trying to deposit her safely on the floor, she wrapped her arms around our necks. The way she smelled was intoxicating. Holding on to us, she said, "Don't put me down yet. I'm in no hurry, guys."

Our hands met under her as we made a basket for her to sit on, Chuck holding on to her tightly with his left arm, his useless right arm dangling by his side. "We can't carry you too far in this small room," Chuck said. We started to swing her and she laughed.

"Where do you want to land?" I asked her.

"Since there's no hay in this room, boys, put me over there," she indicated the darkest corner of the room, behind a counter.

"I saw you guys at the movies in Burlington, but you left before I had a chance to talk to you," she said, making herself comfortable in our arms. "Your names are Chuck and Dick, isn't that right? My name's Margie."

Before we reached the corner of the room, Chuck had to let go of her, making me lose my balance. Tumbling to the floor behind the counter, Margie ended on top of me, her wide skirt covering me.

"Oh, Dick," she said, moving her face close to mine

and wrapping her arm around Chuck's neck, "what shall we do now that we're in this hell of a fix?"

"It's up to you, but whatever you want to do, we won't tell," Chuck said, bending down and pressing himself against her.

"You naughty boys," she laughed, jumping up. "Why don't I put on a little show for you?" She proceeded to pull up her skirt and began making slow, grinding pelvic gyrations and thrusts into the air while Chuck and I drooled. Chuck moved toward the door and peeked through the Venetian blind that protected the room from the prying eyes of students in the crowded corridor.

"You scared of being caught, eh?" she snickered, as she mounted a climactic hurling of her pelvis toward us.

"You're just a beautiful tease, that's all," Chuck said. "But I bet you won't put out the real stuff."

She stopped her provocative dance and began to unbutton her blouse.

"Not here," I said, "where some starry-eyed journalist might come in any minute. It's safer if we go to the chapel in the afternoon. It's empty at that time."

"You guys are crazy," she said with a tone of admiration.

The three of us left the room but agreed to meet in the chapel at two o'clock. It was usually empty in the afternoon and the heavy, main entrance was never locked. There was a padded bench in front of the altar where people knelt while getting saved. It was on that padded, low bench, that Margie dared me to fornicate while Chuck stood by the door guarding the entrance. Later on, we switched around and I guarded. If someone were to appear on the steps, the one guarding was to start whistling the old hymn, "He's Coming Soon."

Nobody came up those steps throughout the whole afternoon while Chuck and I took our turns. I definitely enjoyed the loss of my virginity. Margie was just like Alvin's bitch.

26

During my junior year I tried to convince the college administrators to establish a radio station run by students. Armed with the powerful words from *Revelation* 11:15 about the seventh angel announcing the new kingdom of our Lord, I suggested that the radio station be named "The Angel's Voice." I put the project on its feet, designed the gamut of programs it was to broadcast and chose the announcers, all under the tedious scrutiny of Professor Francken.

After the initial struggles, Francken turned over the operation to me, since it was taking too much of his time. My special interview programs buttered up faculty members and administrators, giving them air space to satisfy their insatiable craving for incessant bragging about their ideas and accomplishments and their wish to be known as devoted Christians.

Chuck Wagner and I also used the radio station for our private commercial purposes by advertising the books we were trying to sell. Advertising was almost free—we volunteered to donate ten percent of our take to the college, a charge we passed on to the consumer as packaging and mailing expenses.

But neither the radio station nor the several projects that followed could have come to fruition had it not been for what I learned by taking a course called Religious Psychology of Personal Adjustment and Improvement. The prof for that class used Dale Carnegie's *How to Win Friends and Influence People*. *The Prince* by Machiavelli—the excommunicated Florentine politician and writer of the Renaissance—was another required reading.

Shortly after I began the course, I talked Chuck into taking it too, certain that it would help him become a better businessman. Under the influence of those two books, I labored to get the initial funds for "The Angel's Voice" project in Syracuse, Albany, Burlington, Montpelier and other smaller towns in the region. Donations started pouring in, much to the delight of H. C.'s administrators, who were forever in search of new schemes to bring in more money. Of course, being in charge of the stash coming in, I made sure some of it got filtered, but the college administrators were so happy with what they received—a gift from Heaven, they called it—that they never suspected I was short-changing them.

"We have never had such an outpouring of support from the larger community," Francken declared at a daily meeting of faculty and students at the chapel. "Much of it is due to the witnessing and effort by Richard Dink," he went on, indicating to me to stand up. Consistent with what I had learned in psych class, I closed my eyes, lifted a hand and told the audience, "All I know comes from the teachings I am receiving here at Heighman College, praying always to increase the Lord's work... and its treasure here on earth." A loud Amen greeted my declaration.

Even though I was entrenched in my position directing the fortunes of "The Angel's Voice" throughout my junior year, when late spring arrived I was asked by Reverend Wesley to enroll in a pastoral counseling internship. The internship was at a mental hospital in the backwoods of Missouri, ministering to so-called criminally insane patients.

At first, I thought this interruption of my radio enterprise would diminish progress toward my goal of a revivalist, but as it turned out, it was just the kind of experience I needed. My step-grandfather, Old Cadaver, seemed to know all along what was best for me, although his power over my life was definitely annoying me. But I had to wait and tolerate him for a while longer. The time would come when I would free myself of his influence and set my own independent course.

The hospital-prison in Fulton, Missouri, where I was to do my pastoral guidance training, housed two hundred and twenty male inmates. Over one hundred of them had committed homicide; thirty had killed twice. A few were multiple murderers. An assortment of pederasts, rapists, Peeping Toms, exhibitionists, vandals and kidnappers rounded out the population, reflecting the myriad offenses committed by the most colorful assortment of psychotics and misfits one could imagine. As summer approached I was dying of curiosity. Deviant behaviors have always fascinated me.

27

Fulton was a village in the middle of Missouri where a dog's bark could be heard from one end of town to the other. The presence of two colleges brought a measure of prestige to the town. One of them—Westminster College—was where Winston Churchill gave his famous Iron Curtain speech.

The vast state hospital at the outskirts of the village was in step with the traditional snake pits that served in many places throughout the nation as warehouses for the mentally sick. Biggs was the building for the "criminally insane," isolated from the main hospital grounds, where over a thousand psychotic and less severely disturbed patients were housed. Biggs had been recently turned into a maximum-security building after an escape of five dangerous prisoners. The men had overcome the guards on the third floor and used the emergency fire hoses to lower themselves to a wall on the second floor. Using twisted bed sheets tied together as ropes, they descended to the ground outside.

Since the escape, the State had built a twenty-foot high electrified barbed wire fence that encircled Biggs's outer wall, and placed permanent guards armed with machine guns on a couple of new towers overlooking the building. Any male prisoner at the Missouri penitentiary in the capital of the state, Jefferson City, who was considered incorrigible, was sure to be sent to Biggs. It was Missouri's top maximum-security building.

I was assigned to the third floor, the top story of this sealed structure, in one of the three small rooms barely large enough to contain a bookcase, a massive desk and two heavy steel chairs. No decorations graced the brick walls. A barred window allowed the rays of the sinking sun to penetrate in the late afternoons. Rooms like mine were used for examinations and therapy. During the summer I spent there, I felt like I was being fried in an oven.

My monthly salary from the Alliance had been increased to $60, and the hospital had a federal grant for its chaplaincy program, bringing me an additional stipend of $300, plus room, board, medical and laundry services.

I didn't have staff status and had to report every move I made to the poseur who called himself a psychologist after receiving a Master's degree in Education from a third-rate school. The gossips regaled me with the fact that he had been dishonorably discharged from the U.S. Army for conduct unbecoming an officer.

Charles Roland was an unredeemable drunk. He was

my immediate supervisor, and reported to the Alliance's liaison, Doctor Freund, a physician who was the Clinical Director. I could attend staff meetings if the patient discussed had a church affiliation, or if someone from any denomination was interested in him. Freund was so aloof that I got to say only a few words to him at a staff meeting. But his name was often mentioned to me by Roland. "Doctor Freund isn't gonna like what you did, Bud," was one of his often-repeated remarks. Roland's office was on the ground floor of the Biggs building, a room much larger than mine and considerably lighter, cooler and better furnished. Roland shared a bathroom with the Clinical Director.

Doctor Freund was an ex-proctologist who had botched his private practice and found a lower paying but secure job in the state's mental hospital system. Whenever a new prisoner found his way into the facility, Freund's first examination would be a proctological one. Some of the better-educated, sophisticated cynics at the main hospital spoke of his examinations as "a thorough Freundian exploration."

The psychological investigation was conducted by Roland. The cynical critics called it the post-anal test because it followed the proctologist's exploration. Roland administered to his subjects a five-minute Rapid Barranquilla Intelligence Test, even though nobody else in the country used it, invalid and unreliable as it was. In addition, the patient was asked to draw a person, a tree and a house. The future of the inmate depended on Roland's five-minute exam. He enjoyed free associating to these drawings and coming up with all sorts of theories about the perversions the subject had likely indulged in, and made wild guesses as to how the prisoner might misbehave in the future. He called it "my psychoanalysis of the case."

A semi-retired psychiatrist from St. Louis, Doctor Scatterfield, came for a day every two weeks and had responsibility for diagnoses and discharges. After their treatment ended, most of the patients were returned to serve out their sentences at the state penitentiary in Jefferson City. Nobody left within their first two years.

A matronly but attractive social worker, Barbara Munroe, had her office near the entrance to the building and took the initial information about all new inmates. I was startled the first time I met her because the neckline of her tight-fitting red dress was cut so low that I noticed her half-exposed breasts quivering as she moved. In some ways, she reminded me of the two Mildreds. She had a thin, black line drawn over her plucked eyebrows, her face was heavily powdered, and her large lips were painted purple—an incongruous sight in such an austere and foreboding place.

Everything about Barbara was intrusive, including her shrill voice. I saw her walk in and out of wards filled with sex-starved men who had not seen a woman in years, with the large key to the main door of Biggs tied to a string around her bare neck, bouncing from one breast to the other. All eyes were glued to her. One of the inmates caustically mentioned to me that when Barbs walked into his ward—housing twenty-five patients and two male attendants—there were twenty-seven immediate erections.

Freund, Roland, Scatterfield and Barbs were the professional specialists attending to the needs and concerns of the inmates. If a prisoner became ill or suffered an accident and needed special care, a nurse from the main hospital was called in for a brief consult. One could only imagine the caliber of the attendants and orderlies at Biggs. Many had not even finished their elementary education and only worked halftime to supplement their meager incomes earned as unskilled laborers and farmers.

I suspected I had seen my first madman at the institution when I met Roland. After I introduced myself, he said, "I am a psychologist and your supervisor. Don't you forget it. Everything you do here must be OK'd by me first. My name is Charles Roland. Many people who know my work around here call me Doctor Roland. That's how I want you to address me." He continued scrutinizing me and, without blinking, went on. "You may wonder about my name, Bud. The name Roland is that of the mythical hero of the Chanson de Roland of the Charlemagne age. His strength was legendary. We Rolands have the chivalrous spirit of the ancient knights. Maybe you don't know it, Bud, but I am a graduate of the West Point Academy." He paused and took in a deep breath of air.

"It's not easy to get into the Academy. Let me tell you!"

When Roland indicated a chair for me to sit on, I presumed he would follow suit and sit down in the chair behind his desk, but he began pacing the floor instead. He approached me again and stood just a few inches in front of me. I looked up at him and then, while he stared into my face, he let out a definite and prolonged fart. When quiet was again restored, he said, without flinching, "Don't let that scare you, Bud. Flatulence was very prevalent among the early French nobility."

Throwing caution to the foul wind, I came back at him saying, "I understand that not only among the French nobility of your ancestry, *Doctor* Roland, but also among the cronies of the Neanderthal man, farts were most popularly accepted as a means of communication."

"Your sense of unsolicited humor is not, I guarantee, going to save your ass around here!" the humorless jerk blurted out, obviously not used to even mild confrontations.

I quickly realized that the more I could enlarge his tenuous self-esteem through what Shakespeare had referred to as "flattering unction," a most primitive type of what is commonly known in our day and age as ass licking, the easier I could manipulate him. I wanted to have free access to the files of each inmate in order to find out the mistakes which led to them getting caught by the authorities, just in case I needed such knowledge in the future.

Contrary to my expectation, Roland refrained from breaking wind again in my presence. He didn't seem to like me, and he left me alone for the most part, telling me to come in for supervision once a week. Being left alone for the most part made it possible to make many church connections. I got permission from Roland to look into the files when I assured him that the ministers in many churches would hear about his cooperation with ministerial duties.

Three weeks following my arrival, a scandal of the first magnitude broke out at Biggs, something Granny might have called a whopping whacker. Not only did it make the headlines of newspapers in Missouri, but international news services carried the story as well.

Biggs's twenty-two most dangerous psychotic murderers were housed in Ward #7 on the third floor, at the opposite end of a long corridor from where my office was located. Even though most patients were heavily sedated with psychotropic drugs just in case they might act out, Ward #7 was manned by the five strongest guards in the hospital. I had paid several visits there to get acquainted with the attendants who were in closest contact with the inmates. It was my duty to relay messages between the inmates and preachers in their communities. The rules of Ward #7 were the most arbitrary in the institution. And they were strictly enforced.

Inmates of Ward #7 were taken only once per week to a large enclosed field on the ground floor to exercise for fifty minutes. The rest of the time they were either in their cells or watching TV in a crowded room, seated in a semi-circle. Each inmate had an assigned chair, which was set at all times on the same, marked spot. Nobody could get up without raising a hand to ask permission to move, or to speak. If one of the four legs of any of the twenty-two chairs were not on the exact spot assigned, marked by a small circle of white chalk, the attendant in charge would yell at the top of his voice, "Put your fucking chair on the right spot or you'll lose five points!" The whole social structure of the institution functioned on the basis of a point system, where inmates got rewarded or punished by gaining or losing points.

When the consultant, Doctor Scatterfield—who kept his eyes closed much of the time, appearing to snooze during staff meetings—was asked if such a behavior modification technique was applicable at Biggs, he deigned to murmur after a long pause, "Use whatever works."

One patient watching TV was mumbling incoherently to himself and had been assigned to sit behind a post. Whenever he'd move his chair around the post in order to see the TV set, the head guard would yell, "Hey, Stuart, you asshole behind the post, move your butt back where it belongs if you know what's good for you!" I was told that Stuart had been trying to look around that post for over three months but the guard would not allow him to change his position. The only way he could peek at a program was by bending around the post while remaining seated. Stuart was a slightly built, middle-aged farmer who had gone berserk, losing his thin thread of sanity while drunk during a New Year's party at a striptease joint in Kansas City, and killing three of the dancers with two well-aimed bullets for each of his favorite ones, to rid himself forever of what had become for him an unbearable temptation.

Stuart's job on the ward was to bring up a cart with the meals from the kitchen on the main floor. He got ten points each time he delivered breakfasts, lunches or dinners for the patients on his ward, but he'd lose most of the points he'd accumulated by the demerits he received in the TV room, reducing his life to a state where he had hardly any privileges. The meals, in two large buckets, were placed on the cart he pushed to the elevator. Often, the chief guard and tormentor made his presence known in the kitchen, repeatedly demeaning Stuart and the other inmates, ordering them to carry out duties they were already in the process of accomplishing routinely.

One Sunday at dinnertime, when there were fewer personnel in the building, Stuart, as usual, came out of the elevator with the steaming buckets into Ward #7. His fellow inmates were waiting their turn for soup that a guard doled out to each with a large ladle. As the level of the soup in the large bucket decreased, the guard in charge noticed that there was something solid and slippery at the bottom of the container. He tilted it to see the contents better, and suddenly the head of the chief guard splashed out of the bucket and rolled on the table where some of the inmates were already eating.

Stuart didn't utter a word from that day on. Mute as a catatonic doornail, an evanescent smile was imprinted forever on his face. An investigation revealed that, while in the kitchen, he had struck the chief guard on the head from behind with a rolling pin, rendered him unconscious, and then proceeded to chop his head off with a meat cleaver that had been left unsecured by a cook. For hours they searched for the body—on every floor, including the elevator shaft. They finally found it stuffed at the bottom of a huge freezer in the kitchen's storeroom, concealed under several sides of frozen beef.

A committee arrived at Biggs from the state legislators in Jefferson City to study the conditions at Biggs. They showed no concern for a dozen children between twelve and fifteen, who had committed minor offenses but were labeled incorrigible and dangerous, and imprisoned at Biggs under the constant influence of hardened criminals, psychopaths with five-page-long psychiatric histories, including all varieties of morbid sexual deviations. The only recommendation the legislators made was to put a new coat of paint on the building.

My first impulse at witnessing this type of horrific neglect was to make myself look like a justice defender by exposing the inhumane treatment reigning inside a Missouri institution. My idea was to report what I saw to the most socially responsible newspaper with a worldwide reputation, the one founded by Joseph Pulitzer, the St. Louis Post-Dispatch. However, my path, I concluded, must be a darker but powerful one. Good reformers usually don't reach the top of the economic or political pyramid in the United States. So I bid farewell to Pulitzer and his type of liberal idealism and didn't write the exposé.

It was a time of great uneasiness, not only in the town of Fulton, but in the whole country. The war in Vietnam was raging and there was a possibility of my getting drafted into the army. But, as Doctor Targownikstein predicted after I broke my forearm, my slight handicap kept me from being inducted, much to my disappointment, for I thought that a couple of years as a chaplain during war-time would enhance my future possibilities as an evangelist, help me break my contract with the Alliance, and perhaps serve as a springboard into an easier political career.

To leave a good record of my patriotic intentions, I applied for induction into the various branches of the Armed Forces on three different occasions, each time—as I suspected—receiving a flat rejection.

I made good contacts in Missouri. Many of the preachers had already heard of my family's reputation as evangelists in nearby Kansas, and of Granny's frustrated political efforts. They ordered—through the mail—hundreds of books that Chuck and I sold, after I marked up the price. Unfortunately, Chuck—having just graduated from H. C.—let me know that soon he would be forced to curtail his activities with me since he was too busy applying to graduate schools. His goal was to be admitted to the London School of Economics. I could use his help only until the end of summer. But while he was available we sold plenty of books.

I also accepted requests to preach at other churches. My sermons concentrated on the duty to serve our country. One of the preachers who was about to take a vacation asked me if I could take over his flock for two weeks. I complied and the experience became one of the most productive in Fulton. Alvin had taught me that most church people find it easier to follow an idea they think was initiated by them, so I manipulated the congregation into starting Bingo on Saturdays and made out like a bandit, charging the participants what I called "donations for worthy causes." When the preacher returned, he was happy to find a couple of hundred unexpected dollars in his coffers, while I had taken the bulk of the money.

I invited members who made the greatest donations to a meeting, serving them refreshments and passing out special commendations and tags with their names, which increased their generosity. I figured that everyone likes to feel like a V.I.P., so I made sure the rest of the congregation didn't feel left out by throwing a party everyone could attend.

When my presence in Missouri became known through the evangelical grapevine in nearby Kansas, I received a few invitations from churches in Topeka. My first reaction was to excuse myself, saying I was too busy, remembering Alvin's teachings about how the longer one can hold out, the more they'll want you and the more they'll pay. I held out and received daily telephone invitations, each one with greater inducements, to give a couple of sermons, one of them certain that with extra P. R. about the return of the boy-preacher, they could practically guarantee a full house of over five hundred.

Finally, I accepted three appearances during the weekend of July 4. The host preachers in Topeka were flabbergasted after the meetings concluded when I plunked down $723 in the first preacher's hands, gave $815 to the second preacher, and $1,278 to the third, after skimming off bundles of bills. A large number of parishioners had ordered the colorfully illustrated *Bibles* from Chuck. Before parting, each of the preachers gave me a hundred dollars. I sent a money order for $200 to the Alliance, saying that I wanted to share with them what the preachers had given me.

Before I departed, I found out that Alvin had moved away and was preaching in California. Neither Phyllis nor Mildred showed up during my stay and I didn't care to inquire about them. Good riddance! And as far as Doctor T was concerned, I heard he had become Chief Psychiatrist at the Kansas State Penitentiary in Topeka, but I didn't look him up.

I ran into a gold mine at one of the Topeka churches. After my evening sermon, I noticed an elegantly dressed old gentleman looking in my direction, nervously waiting for me to get untangled from the sheep gathered around me. When I disposed of the parishioners, the old man approached me. Making sure no one was eavesdropping, he put his hand out and touched my shoulder. His gold Rolex watch and a heavy diamond ring on his finger caught my attention. "Reverend," he said, "I have a very sick granddaughter. I'm at the end of my rope trying to get help for her. Nobody knows what's wrong. She's getting worse." He was nearly crying.

I immediately perked up. This might be a terrific opportunity to get my first wealthy backer. I figured he was looking for a miracle and I knew the fantastic incomes that successful spiritual healers received.

"My name is Tommy Waters. I have faith in you after listening to your sermon," he went on. "Just pray for her and she'll get better. You don't even have to place your hands on her and she'll heal. I have faith." Tears rolled down his face onto his neatly starched shirt.

I embraced him and, playing it safe remembering what Granny taught me, I said, "The only one who can perform miracles is God. Your faith will be rewarded the way the centurion's faith was rewarded in the 13th verse of *Matthew*, chapter 8. Go now to your granddaughter."

An hour later, as I was packing my luggage, I received a telephone call from the old man. His voice was elated. "I found her sitting up on her bed with the same smile of her happy childhood on her face. She got up by herself and she's beginning to feel better."

"Your faith and God helped her," was all I said. It's best to say the least number of words and leave things suspended in as much mystery as possible, where the person can project his own wishes and satisfy them according to his needs. Miracles are performed inside the head of the believer, never in reality. If good old Mister Tommy wanted to perceive a miracle and assume his position in the long line of superstitious dumbbells, so be it. And, better still, if he wanted to give me the credit for it.

The next day, Mr. Tommy Waters was waiting for me in the hotel lobby. "She's recovering but I don't want anybody to know about this," he said, handing me a sealed envelope. "Tell no one. This is an anonymous gift to you. Use it for any project you want to undertake, Reverend, and please keep in touch."

I could hardly wait for him to get out of my sight, I was so eager to find out what was in the envelope. It contained the man's card with a note saying, "Keep in touch and bless you Reverend," and a check made out to me for five thousand dollars. It was the first of my big hauls. Of course I kept the card, knowing it might open the doors of my future Fort Knox, where half the gold of the world is stored, and immediately mailed the check, special delivery, to my bank in Canada.

After my return from Topeka, the invitations to preach around Fulton came in steadily on Sundays and often for Wednesday evening prayer meetings as a substitute preacher. Having heard of my success in Topeka, my reputation had grown and I was attracting huge crowds to my sermons. And they were dropping larger offerings. I was mailing money orders to my savings account at the Montréal bank to the tune of $450 a week. People, especially those with few resources, are so ready to reach deep into their pockets. I had recently grown a mustache and the motherly ladies looked at me adoringly, opening their hearts and their purses to me.

Barbs liked my new mustache. She often roamed around the third floor, looking into my office. Once, when we were alone, she stuck her tongue in my ear and then whispered, "That mustache of yours, Dick! It excites me! I'd like to wrap my thighs around it."

I laughed uproariously when I heard that. What a nut, I thought. There was nothing subtle about her.

Barbs brought me professional articles and histories of severely disturbed patients, with batteries of psychological tests that had been administered and analyzed in more reputable places than the State Hospital #1 at Fulton, some of them by experts in St. Louis. I began to study the basic psychological makeup of the various categories of emotional disorders. I was most intrigued by tests like the Rorschach Inkblot and learned the kinds of responses that would indicate emotional disturbance. I wanted to learn how fairly normal individuals responded, as well as the ways to hide pathologies. Another test, the Minnesota Multiphasic Personality Inventory, a long string of true or false questions, had several indexes that revealed whether the person was lying, exaggerating their good qualities, or trying to appear more disturbed than they were. I found an article describing the most normal answers, memorized them, and confirmed what I had suspected all along; in spite of my unusually high level of intelligence, I possessed certain deviant features in my personality, inherited and learned through my family's nuttiness. None of the case histories I read in the files, nor the ones brought by Barbs to seduce me, topped the peculiarities existing in my own family, even though we hadn't hatched a murderer yet.

One late afternoon, when most of the personnel had already left, Barbs intercepted me as I was about to enter the elevator to go down to the dorm at the main hospital where I took my meals and slept.

"What's your hurry?" she said, locking her bare arm around my shoulder. "Everybody's safely tucked away in the wards. The corridors are empty. Let me show you what this crazy perverted lunatic oversexed fiend proposed to me in his letter. You'll find it very interesting."

She pulled me back to my office and gave me the most grotesquely lurid pornographic material one could imagine. "All you have to do," the letter ended, "is come and get me. Say I need some therapy. We can go to that small space next to the conference room after hours, where nobody will see us. Silence is the word. You won't

regret it and I will take our secret to the grave. Promise."
It was signed by an inmate called Frankie.

"Tempting, eh?" Barbs said to me. "Wouldn't you like to have the same kind of pleasures if a woman like me offered them to you? There's a cozy place in Room 305."

It wasn't difficult to let Barbs seduce me. But I wasn't about to flirt with the kind of trouble I might have if caught right next to my office, so I winked at her. "Not here, Barbs," I forced myself to say with difficulty. Several of the patients at Biggs had been caught doing nothing more than engaging in oral sex and were imprisoned for years, diagnosed as criminally insane psychopaths. Clearly, it was too small a prize for taking such high a risk. I sought out a better opportunity.

After enjoying overnight meetings two weekends in a row with Barbs at a cheap motel near Fulton, she asked me several times to meet her again, but I refused. More than twice with the same person creates a dependency I detest.

From a list of all the patients with church affiliations, I discovered that Frankie belonged to a fundamentalist church back home, The Holy Children of God's Tabernacle. I had a special interest in him after I found out that he and Barbs were often meeting in Room 305 late in the evenings. She had formally taken him on as a therapy case.

Frankie was raised in reform schools from which he ran away only, to be caught and punished. He'd been

placed in increasingly secure institutions and finally
sentenced to the penitentiary for assaulting a woman.
To his credit, he passed a high school equivalency test
while in prison and was released after serving four years.
He managed to stay out of trouble working as an opera-
tor at a porno movie house in Kansas City, although
there were periods when he disappeared for months at a
time.

Frankie was apprehended after raping a woman in
Kansas City and taken directly to Biggs, where he had
been incarcerated for six years. But he escaped while un-
dergoing a psychological examination at the main
hospital.

A young woman, without much experience with
dangerous delinquents, asked the guard who had
brought Frankie to her office from Biggs in handcuffs, to
remove them and return to his duties. He misunderstood
her and went back to Biggs. When he returned to get
Frankie, he found the psychologist tied to a radiator.
Frankie had taken a piece of cardboard and made a sign
he tied to the woman's neck, saying in thick caps, "I'M
LUCKY FOR BEING SO UGLY." After taking her car
keys, he drove away. The authorities caught up with
Frankie in New Orleans a year later and brought him
back to Biggs, where he spent another five years.

Two psychiatric reports underestimated the severity
of Frankie's disturbance, saying he harbored anti-social
attitudes, but emphasizing his high level of intelligence,

good verbal capacities, and his personal tidiness. A third report, the most extensive, was based on various interviews and the aid of psychological diagnostic test evaluations. Frankie was described as "a malignant narcissistic psychopath with a personality disorder of a paranoid nature, capable of extreme antisocial and disorganized thinking and behavior, such as manifested in pathologies with underlying inordinately destructive and sadistic impulses." An ominous and specific warning stood out in the report like a red flag in the section headed Prognosis. "The chaotic emotions in this patient are likely to surface without warning and explode, especially toward women."

At the end of the summer, I saw Frankie in the corridor by my office, ready to be escorted down to the conference room for a review of his case before the staff to determine if he should be released to the community. Barbs had scheduled him for a meeting with the expert from St. Louis, Doctor Scatterfield.

Fattened by years of physical inactivity, the consultant sat with his eyes half-closed at the head of a long table, chewing on a pencil. He seemed bored as Barbs regaled the staff with glowing accounts of her successful therapeutic activities with Frankie.

"I've treated him three to four times a week for the past two-and-a-half months, an hour each session," Barbs went on. Scatterfield barely opened one eye, tilting his head up as he quizzically looked at her.

"And did the poor fellow survive your treatment, Barbs?" he mumbled. She giggled, coyly saying something about how funny Doctor Scatterfield was, and went on to explain the changes that had taken place in Frankie's attitude, adding that he had become interested in reading the *Bible*. She also made sure the file contained Frankie's statement about how he had been saved and had found Christ while in the hospital. Cured by the Holy Spirit and Barbs!

I've never known it to fail—whenever a person invokes God to convince me that he's on the right path and will never again commit a crime, I know he's a liar.

While Barbs talked, Frankie's folder was passed around the table. I leafed through it and realized that the damaging report with the terrible prognosis was missing. I looked at Barbara intensely and saw her discomfort. She could tell I had read that report. She stared at me and I recognized the same kind of threat in her look that had been in Phyllis's eyes during our father's burial.

Doctor Freund and Roland backed Barbara's recommendation to return Frankie to the community. After a brief discussion, Frankie was called into the room. Looking much younger than his years, wearing wide-rimmed glasses, his blond hair falling casually over his blue eyes, relaxed, tall and handsome, he made a good impression. The other inmates called him Baby-Face. At the end of the meeting, Scatterfield said Frankie should be released.

Six months after my experience at Biggs, safely in

my senior year at Heighman College, I received a newspaper clipping stating that Frankie had violated his parole by assaulting a woman and was returned to Biggs. Barbs was fired and forced out of social work.

Shortly afterwards, Frankie killed a young woman with a broomstick on the same corridor where my office had been. She was described as the most brilliant student in her medical school graduating class, and was just beginning her psychiatric residency at Biggs. Freund and Scatterfield managed to retain their positions.

Roland continued drinking heavily until one day he locked himself in his office, gulped down a fifth of whiskey, passed out and never woke up. He was supposed to be out on his two-week vacation. The stench emanating from his office led to the discovery of his remains. An autopsy revealed that he had mixed a generous portion of a deadly poison in his favorite bourbon.

28

For the rest of my life I remembered that every day I spent at Biggs I was most grateful that I could leave the premises. Freedom was and would always be my most important possession, and my experience at that horrible place served as a constant reminder that I had to find ways to succeed without risking it. I had studied the folders of nearly all the patient-prisoners at the maximum-security hospital throughout the summer. I found that most of them had been labeled as psychotic, psychopathic, or both.

Psychopaths, I learned from the report about Frankie that was missing from his folder, are good at covering up their innermost deficiencies, remaining undiagnosed as such and are labeled instead as having anti-social tendencies.

With Frankie as an example, most psychopaths are detected only when they are involved in a bizarre criminal activity, showing the disorganized and irrational behavior of a paranoid nature. What I had intuitively arrived at on how I should live my life was confirmed by the case reports I read. Even if in the future I felt like murdering—and there might be good reason to do so in order to reach my goals—I'd do it without flinching and in such a way that nobody would ever suspect me. I would not depend on anyone's protection to conceal my crime. But I'd rather outwit the victim, get rid of him or her by finding their secret weakness, and cause them public ruin. Then I would take over.

My high intellectual capacities would carry me through to success. I admire and envy the power of the Caesars, the Borgia popes, the Caligulas, Hitlers, and Stalins of human history. But often their greed blinded them and brought their empires and their lives to dust. They were poor psychopaths, not knowing how to cover their pathology.

It's hard for a man with my background, with my internal and well-hidden personality disfigurations and impulses, to control myself. I get bored unless there's action. Something interesting and exciting—if not downright peculiar—has to happen to me all the time or I feel I will come apart.

I find it exhilarating when there's trouble around me, when I am in the center of the fray, when I get to master the situation and come out winning, get what I want, when I want it. Daring to do what others fear is half the fun in my life. But being stupid is worse than daring and failing. Stupidity is something I can't tolerate in myself. Disarm with charm, is my motto.

I believe I live among vipers that are ready to devour

me or, at least, destroy my plans. The only way to live is to try to take advantage of them first, before they bite. The best way I can carry out my plans is by being a religious or political leader. That is the way most of those I admire have succeeded. Through religion it might be easier to carry out my plans because the large masses are so needy that they are ready to follow one who promises a golden and infinite future called Paradise. Just look at how those Catholic and Moslem leaders work over their followers! But I must stay very alert because it's precisely there—among religious and political leaders—where the nests of the most dangerous vipers are found.

Competition among psychopaths is most difficult.

To achieve ultimate power, mix religion and politics. That's where most of the truly great psychopaths are found, but very seldom unmasked. I will be among them and already know for certain that the only way to succeed among them is to be the best in knowing the clever ways to always hide behind God.

29

I got more trouble than I needed just before leaving Fulton in my Chevy. I received a letter from Margie. It sent a chill up my spine, knowing that if I didn't properly manage the conflict she posed I might get expelled from H. C. and all my plans for the spectacular career I had envisioned would surely flounder. Her short note said she had missed two periods and was pregnant. "Either you or Chuck would be the Daddyooo, since nobody else visited," she joked.

God only knew how many others she had enticed. But whether it was me or Chuck, didn't really matter. All she had to do was to accuse us and we would be in deep shit. I cursed myself for being so stupid. My first thought was to get rid of her, kill her, if necessary, but I curbed my impulse. I smiled to myself, as I confirmed how my most immediate reaction had so obviously been like that of a psychopath. But I wasn't among the ones whose main discharge of impulses had to be a violent one. I was more like a parasite that sucks out the life of its victim. The possibility of total violence should be used only to

resolve a transcendental problem of worldwide conse-
quences, not the trivial problem brought on by a pregnant
girl. My pathology was better defended, more hidden, and
therefore much more malignant and dangerous.

I phoned Margie and said I was on my way. "I'll be
there day after tomorrow," I assured her, "and will take
care of everything. Don't worry. I know a man in Montréal
who'll help us end the problem."

Margie seemed relieved.

Not to arouse suspicions at Heighman, we decided
to meet at one of the motels in Burlington, Vermont.

I arrived late at night on my second day of driving.
Margie was waiting, looking radiant. After our long separation, she was more aroused than usual. But I was already
thinking ahead about other, more important matters. I was
no longer interested in her and began thinking of her as
plain "M," and thinking about getting as far away from her
as possible, name and all.

I had seen many peculiar clients in Mr. Lepinski's
jewelry and pawnshop in Montréal, people who placed
bets with him for horse races, and was sure he'd know
someone who would direct us to a reliable abortionist.

We returned to Heighman after our successful mission in Montréal—definitely rid of what might have been
Chuck's or my offspring—and I began to see less of M,
intending to end the relationship. After my experience at
Biggs, and the incident with M, I was jolted into a new
reality. I had to be more careful.

My senior year was the most profitable of my four years at Heighman. I had more time to follow my own interests because the extra credits I had earned during the previous two summers were almost sufficient to let me graduate. All I needed were a couple of reading courses with Francken.

A few weeks into my senior year, after sustaining a short correspondence with my wealthy admirer in Topeka, Mr. Tommy Waters, the future of my career was sketched out when he arranged to meet me. He wanted to promote me for having saved his granddaughter's life, or so he said—a notion I didn't want to dispute even though I thought he must be very superstitious, believing in such fanciful explanations.

After listening to several broadcasts of "The Angel's Voice," Tommy Waters instructed an agency to find a radio station for sale in New York State. I received a letter and the bill of sale for a radio station in Syracuse, New York. I signed and sent the dollar he asked for, which he said he was going to frame and display in his study. It was a small station but with excellent equipment that transmitted over a long distance. My programs reached as far south as Harrisburg, Pennsylvania; north to Québec; west to Cleveland; east to Boston. That was a big slice of the country and a great beginning.

I hired a couple of students as helpers to pack and mail books, and keep lists of buyers to target as future contributors. I found out that the surest way to make contributors out of listeners was to give them a chance to call on the telephone and let them witness for the Lord on the radio, establishing with them a personal relationship. They felt that being on the air was a mystical event, a spiritual sort of approximation to the invisible throne of God. Once hooked, they sent money, and continued sending money for years, putting me in their wills to nail down their salvation.

The gullibility of ignorant people in need, wanting to tell the world about their family background, their dreams and craving for human fellowship, or to receive a few words of comfort, never ceases to amaze me. I kept special lists of those who sent me less than two dollars, of those who sent money more than once, and mailed different letters of acknowledgement and thanks to each group. Like arrows hitting their targets. I carried those lists for years in my pocket and memorized thousands of names in case I'd meet them. When that would happen, I'd just about floor them when they realized I remembered their full names. And then they really emptied their wallets. It never failed.

My *Summa Cum Laude* graduation at H. C. was an event that would not be forgotten for a long time. I showed everybody a bit of class and luxury. Since my savings account, which I had kept fattening every week, had grown to over fifty thousand dollars, I thought it was high time to fulfill a wish I'd had ever since Alvin told me that what really impresses people are the clothes one wears and the car one drives. The poor devil, as clever as he was, never could sate his ambition for funds. Since I had money while I was still young, I went on a buying spree just before my graduation. First, Mr. Lepinski sold me a large and ostentatious emerald, mounted on a huge platinum ring surrounded by small diamonds that would put anyone's eye out, for half the marked-up price. It was the centerpiece in the exhibit of his showcase. I knew he was still making a good profit, but didn't care. Since most of the successful preachers in those days drove big, black cars, I went to Buffalo, to an agency near Niagara Falls, and traded my Chevy for a new white Lincoln Continental, the most elegant car I had ever set eyes on. It drove like a dream.

Next, I got a wardrobe fit for British royalty. Extraordinarily conservative. That's how I celebrated my twenty-first birthday! When I returned to the college all decked out, I could tell I had made a wild impression on Heighmaniacs.

Professor Francken confronted me, puzzled about my new appearance. I repeated what my mother said when asked by nosy church congregants about her gaudy way of dressing. I said, "I want to show the difference between the drab way people dress and what I wear, so more attention will be paid to how the Lord calls me to witness for Him."

He just smiled. The benevolent idiot!

My next move was to talk Granny into persuading

Old Cadaver to allow me to buy my way out of the contract with WACO for twenty grand.

For a graduation gift I received more than half a million dollars from the one hundred thousand listeners, whose names and addresses I treasured in the safety of the bank's vault. I had been personally keeping in touch with each one throughout my entire career as revivalist: I called them my base. I was a free man and TV was still taking off.

My last encounter with Mr. Ernst took place three years after my graduation at Heighman, when I was asked by professor Francken to deliver the Commencement address. When Mr. Ernst saw me on the campus, he rushed toward me and with tears running down his cheeks dropped to the ground on his knees and pled, "Get *really* saved, Dicky. You can fool the world, but an old foxy gambler like me can tell you haven't been born again. Get saved, Dicky, for your own good, before it's too late."

Two weeks later, I followed his admonition and was born again on my knees, crying this time hot and visible tears, when I held a revival meeting before a full house at Madison Square Garden in New York City, where I confessed a very select batch of minor sins to impress my audience of sheep.

EPILOGUE

First page notice in international newspapers:
"At the age of sixty-three, the Reverend Doctor
Richard Dink was an unstoppable force during the Republican presidential convention in New York City,
when he lent his support and fortune 'to save the country
from Democrat abuses,' as he put it. Reverend Dink's
nomination by his party for the Vice Presidency—
demanded by many right-wing editorials and over 10,000
vehement bloggers—was assured when he flashed out of
his vest pocket, in his usual flamboyant and charmer's
style, a red check book, and wrote a check for two billion
dollars, with a 'b,' not an 'm.' 'For starters,' he said with a
smile—to support the candidacy of fellow Republicans
running for office, the largest private, political donation
on record.

"Since the law that limits ownership of radio stations
to forty (by one single person or corporation) was repealed
in 1966 by the Federal Communications Commission, the
reverend was able to accumulate 1,243 radio stations inside
the borders of the United States, and 165,379 billboards

promoting them—with well over twenty million contributing followers whose votes he vowed to deliver.

"One of the wealthiest men in the world according to most surveys, he is the clearest and most vehement voice for the religious far right, responsible to a large extent for the blurring between State and Church that was launched in the second administration of born-again George W. Bush. Richard Dink became the darling of conservatives with his slogan 'No separation between Church and State!'

"For the last twenty years, he has been one of the main proponents for the abolition of abortion, backing the election of over twenty conservative senators and several prominent governors, countless members of the House of Representatives, state assemblymen, and a multitude of other politicians up and down the political pyramid.

"After he received the nomination, Dink was heard bragging to some of his colleagues: 'As long as we're able to convince the voters that we are the true defenders of family values and morality—and we continue to have approval from our pals in the Supreme Court to Gerrymander in every state and receive unlimited amounts of money from the conservative industrialists—we'll stay in power indefinitely.'

"Only a few Republicans tried in vain to block his nomination, daring to raise questions that have plagued the career of Rev. Dink, including accusations of several

prostitutes that have surfaced from time to time; his obscure dealings in the emerald market of Colombia that
many say he used to wash money in cahoots with the
drug lords in Mexico; and his highly controversial program of 'Adoption Not Abortion' for Latin American
countries, tied by many to the illicit market of babies.

"Since none of the accusations were proved in court,
it was futile to try to stop the GOP from nominating him.
Those who had serious questions about Rev. Dink finally
gave in when they were assured that, if elected, his duties
as Vice President would be minimal and mainly re-
stricted to the newly appointed Office of Religious
Affairs in the White House. They were convinced that
Dinky would never become President."

Characters, in their order of appearance

The Reverend Sister Elberta Todd, aka Granny or Grandmother.

Richard Dink, aka Dink or Dinky, preacher, and main protagonist.

Doctor Targownikstein, aka The Psychiatrist or Doctor T.

Reverend James Paul Dink, aka Preacher Dad, P. D., or Dad.

Phyllis, Dinky' half-sister.

Mildred, Dinky's Mom; Granny's daughter.

Alvin S. Grabbe, substitute preacher and Dinky's role model.

Floye, Phyllis's mother.

Reverend Doctor Bean, pastor of the Light of the Holy Ghost Church.

Juan Pablo Javier Vargas Merino de la Torre, Phyllis's beau.

Reverend Doctor Wesley Neighbour, missionary and violinist.

Mildred, the prostitute in New York City.

Mr. Ernest Ernst, printer, missionary, and billiards champion.

Mrs. Laura Schmickel, college bursar.

Miss Valentina Gradzkikiviana, or Valy Gradz, or Vicky Grass.

Roberto López, or Bob, fellow student from Perú, and Vicky's beau.

Mrs. Lucille Davies, pioneer missionary to Africa.

Chuck Wagner, Dinky's only college pal.

Jesús Lehman, student book salesman and cheap cheat.

Reverend Doctor Francken, Dean of the college and professor.

Mr. Vayda, movie house owner, collaborator of "The Underground."

Reverend Wagner, Chuck's father.

Reverendo Don Julio Bolivar, converted priest in Colombia.

Reverend Doctor & Mrs. Douglas and Bobby, Jr., family of missionaries.

Dolores, the black prostitute in Ratonpelao, Colombia.

Rodrigo Restrepo, student preacher enamored of the USA in Medellín.

Andy Michaels, accountant at a print shop in Medellín.

José Vieira Cano, or Pepe, the *Marrano* from Colombia.

Margie, floozy co-ed at Heighman College, New York.

Doctor Scatterfield, psychiatric consultant at the hospital-prison in Fulton, Missouri.

Doctor Freund, clinical director of the madhouse at Fulton, Missouri.

Charles Roland, drunken supervisor at Fulton's mental hospital.

Stuart, the decapitator at Fulton State Hospital #1 in Fulton.

Barbara Munroe, or Barbs, seductress social worker at Fulton State Hospital.

Frank, the killer, and protector and lover of Barb in Fulton.

Mr. Lepinski, the Canadian jeweler and gambler in Montréal.

Mr. Tommy Waters, multimillionaire, Dinky's first big donor.

About the Author

ANDRÉS BERGER-KISS was born in Szombathely, Hungary, into a family of actors and poets, spent is early childhood in Holland, but grew up in the Andes and jungles of Colombia, South America, where his family fled to escape the methodical extermination of Jews. He moved to New York for undergraduate studies, earned his Masters in psychology from Indiana University, and was awarded a doctorate in psychology from the University of Missouri. He worked as a clinical psychologist, including two years at the Menninger Clinic, and taught psychology at the university level. He was chief psychologist and director of Mental Health Education for the State of Oregon when he decided to devote himself fulltime to writing.

Berger-Kiss has published three novels, two books of poetry, and one book of short stories. He is co-author of a film script for "The Sharpener" based on his prize-winning short story. Other work has appeared in numerous anthologies of poetry, short stories and essays published in the United States, Colombia, Mexico, Puerto Rico, Hungary, and Spain, including *Best Latino Short Stories of the Decade,* published by the University of Houston, and *Best International Short Stories,* published by Europa Press in Budapest. Andres Berger-Kiss has given 289 recitals of his poetry in three continents.

Earnings from his literary efforts are sent to the Guavio Elementary School in Bogotá, Colombia, to assist the children.